D1617016

MAR 23 '81	DATE DUE	
JAN 30 '82		
OV 27 199		
OCT 30 1991		
APR 24 1993		
FEB 19 1997		
APR 10 2000		
SEP 24 2002		
AUG 11 2004		
OCT 19 2004		
DEC 26 2007		

F
Ree   Reese, John   27889

             Dead eye

DISCARD
Wrangell Public Library

Irene Ingle Public Library
P.O. Box 679
Wrangell, Alaska 99929

Dead Eye

Also by John Reese

Dead Eye

JOHN REESE

DOUBLEDAY & COMPANY, INC.

GARDEN CITY, NEW YORK

1978

27889

All of the characters in this book are fictitious, and
any resemblance to actual persons, living or dead, is
purely coincidental.

Library of Congress Cataloging in Publication Data

Reese, John Henry.
Dead eye.

I. Title.
PZ3.R25673De   [PS3568.E43]   813'.5'4

ISBN: 0-385-13396-0
Library of Congress Catalog Card Number 77–78514

Copyright © 1978 by John Reese
All Rights Reserved
Printed in the United States of America
First Edition

For

LEE and CAROLYN GORKA,
booksellers who face the
one-eyed monster of TV
fearlessly, and keep people
reading. May their tribe
increase!

Dead Eye

CHAPTER ONE

Straight as a taut string ran this part of the Great Northern, but the buttes were not far ahead. A late spring snow, wet, heavy, and worth its weight in gold to the cattlemen, obscured most of the train to the shabby-looking brakeman who kept watch in the cupola on the caboose. His face, heavily covered with a scruffy brown beard, creased in a slight smile under his wide-brimmed black hat as he listened to the conductor bawling out a brakeman down below.

"No goddamn boomer sasses me back!" the conductor was snarling. "Next stop, you git out and ride the front end, and I don't mean in the injin, neither! I want you up in front of it, on the pilot, until this goddamn storm clears up."

The brakeman had the guts to talk back. "A man can't see no more from the pilot than you can from the engineer's seat," he said.

"He can if the goddamn injineer is stone blind like this sonofabitch," the conductor raged. "When we take water at Pekay Junction, you git up there on the pilot and you stay there till I tell you otherwise."

"You and Jim Hill can take the Great Northern and—" The brakeman broke off suddenly.

Silence, as the creak and rumble of the caboose

drowned out the sound of the blow of the conductor's fist and the thud of the brakeman's body as he went down. The Great Northern, perhaps more than any other railway, relied on "boomer" train crews, men who took one trip at a time, who felt loyalty to no line, who worked all of them as the need or notion inspired them. A conductor could indeed have trouble with a two-boomer crew like this one.

But this conductor was going to have trouble with any crew, wherever he went, because he was big as a house, brutal as a bull, and so ignorant he had trouble keeping his own train's timecard. The man in the cupola had been doing most of his writing for him since last night. It was now almost noon, and the stew bubbling on the cast-iron stove down below was almost done.

There was the sound of another scuffle, and the man in the cupola looked down and saw the gigantic conductor dragging the brakeman by the collar to the ladder.

"Git up there and top-watch. London, take holt of this worthless bastard and drag him up there to help you out," he said.

The man in the cupola leaned down and caught the half-conscious brakeman by the shoulders of his jacket. He gave a heave, and the man slumped into the other seat, where he would be riding backward.

"Turn him around, London," the conductor said. "He can't see nothing there."

"You go to hell, fatty," the man in the cupola said genially. "When I'm riding the top in a snowstorm, I want to know what's up ahead. This fella can't see his finger in front of his nose."

"I give the orders on this train and—"

"You sure do," London cut in. "Too damn many of them. You want to take this train on to the division point all by yourself, just keep shooting off your big fat mouth."

London could see the conductor staring up at him, full of fury, ready to beat on him as he had beaten on the man still slouched on the other seat. But weight and size were no advantage when a man had to climb an iron ladder to get to his prey and then fight in a glass-walled, four-by-four compartment almost filled by two seats.

London knew that the conductor had an old Colt .45 in his office, as his corner desk was called, but this was not the place to use it. He could threaten with it to his heart's content, but he was already shorthanded and if he killed or crippled a man he would be just that much worse off.

And he knew it. He muttered something and vanished, and London leaned back and watched the man draped across the other seat. The conductor obviously had caught him a good one on the jaw, and he was out like a light.

Well, nothing to do but wait. He opened his sheepskin coat and made sure of his own .45, which he wore in a holster of his own design. It clipped to the belt that held his pants up so that the gun lay almost horizontally. A spring pawl in the holster gripped the front sight so that it would never fall out, yet a slight twist freed it.

It was the fastest way he knew to get a gun out, and many a time it had saved his life. He also carried a little .32 in a shoulder holster that was big enough for a .38. The .38 was too bulky, too easily detected, in the close quarters of the caboose.

While the other brakeman still slept, London took from his hip pocket a limber, shot-filled leather sap and put it in his shirt pocket, under his coat. This was really his favorite weapon, and he was an artist with it. You could kill or simply knock a man out with it. You could maim him temporarily or permanently, if you knew how.

He was a man who could have been anywhere from thirty-five to fifty, of average height but with good shoulders and arms, and without an ounce of fat on him. His narrow, hazel eyes flicked about continuously under his battered old hat, observing everything. Under the month's growth of scruffy brown beard was concealed a mustache, that much was clear.

It was also clear that he was no ordinary boomer. He had made the crew aware of this before the train left the station. He had come aboard with two pieces of luggage, to which the big conductor had objected. "Get rid of one or the other," he had said. "You go to hell," the boomer had replied. "If you're crowded, take about thirty pounds of lard off your fat gut."

The conductor doubled up his fist. The boomer held up a warning finger.

"Better think it over, fella," he said. "You're one man short as it is. Either I come aboard with my bags or you whistle out of town with one brakie. Or what'll you bet I can go down to the trainmaster's office and come back with the conductor's assignment myself. Like to call my bluff?"

That had been that.

The train rocked on. It was not really cold, and this snowstorm, while it might bring a lot of precious moisture to the cattle range, was not going to drift. The only danger was that it obscured everybody's vision.

The engineer up in front of the forty-car train had the

most responsibility. How could he see a broken rail under six inches of snow? Suppose a herd of hungry cattle started across the tracks? He could be into them before he knew it, and many an engine had been derailed by piling up too many dead critters before it could be stopped.

The Great Northern's roadbed had never been anything to brag about. The contractors had built good bridges, but in between them they had built fast by building cheaply. The lack of ballast under and between the ties made the rails sink and rise under the train, and this undulation coud derail an empty or lightly loaded car anywhere in the train.

It was the top watch's job to keep an eye out for such "bouncers" and yank the brake cord the moment one looked ready to "dance off," as they said. He also watched for hot boxes. The boxcar bearings were big journals that turned in journal boxes packed with oil-soaked rag waste. If they ran short of oil, friction could set the waste afire. The bearing could overheat and seize up, or burst into flames that could set the whole train afire. It had happened.

Thus, at every stop a trainman went down each side of the train, in one hand an iron rod a couple of feet long with a hook on the end of it, and in the other hand a big can of oil. With the hook he opened the spring-loaded door of each journal box. In most cases he also felt it with his bare hand. If it looked dry or felt warm, he poured in oil. If he found one ready to burst into flames, flagmen were sent out to protect both ends of the train while the rest of the crew poured water into the journal box to cool it down.

Then it had to be packed with oil-soaked waste again,

and the waste tamped in with the same iron hook used to open the door, before the train could proceed. The Great Northern, like other railroads, did not like delays. Conductors who had delays caught hell and might even be reduced to brakemen without steady jobs who had to boom their way home on some other line.

〰〰〰

It was not an easy job, but the bearded, seedy man in the cupola did it well. He was also an excellent portrait artist with crayons, a crack shot with either long or short gun, a coldblooded gambler who rarely lost and who knew every crooked dealer west of the Missouri, and a masseur of considerable skill.

Although the conductor knew him as Zeke London, his name was Jefferson Hewitt and in the plainest terms he was a private detective. Actually he was a partner in a firm called Bankers Bonding and Indemnity Company of Cheyenne, Wyoming. The other partner was an accountant, a fastidious and often pompous German immigrant, well educated, and a genius at finance. The firm bonded corporation and public officials, Conrad writing the bonds and Hewitt doing the field investigation that was necessary.

Hewitt spent most of his time, however, on private cases, both civil and criminal, that brought in more and more of the firm's income. He spoke Spanish, German, French, and Italian well enough to get by. He dressed well and was as much at home in the eastern cities as on his own beat, which was everything west of the Missouri.

He was a man's man who liked women without being obsessed by them, and women liked him even when they knew—some of them, anyway—that he was not a marrying man.

He had come out of the Ozarks a near-illiterate boy who had to lie about his age to join the Army. He did not envy the officers their rank and privileges—only their education. He began reading books—a book a day, sometimes ten a week—until the time came when he felt at home with any officer of any rank. He aspired only to be a corporal and a company clerk, but he became what many officers called "the best damned company clerk in this man's Army."

He served almost five years at the Presidio in San Francisco. He was there during the riots that narrowly missed being recorded in Army annals as a mutiny. A tough general who assumed personal command during the crisis called him in for confidential testimony because, as he said, "When I want to know what the hell is really going on, Corporal, I ask the company clerk."

The company clerk's name was then Hugh Goff, and he was able, in a few words, to give the general the damning information on a few officers who were responsible for the trouble. One was cashiered, another permitted to resign his commission. Corporal Goff was offered a chance to enter the academy and become an officer himself.

When he refused, the general agreed that he was basically a loner and not really "officer material." But he knew of a good job with the Pinkerton Agency and would send him there with an honorable discharge containing his personal citation.

He stayed with Pinkerton for several years, until a

Cheyenne bank offered to back him and Conrad Meuse in BB&I. He had used many names working as a private investigator, and now he was working for the Great Northern as Zeke London.

But for years he had used the name Jefferson Hewitt until today it was his own. He was a self-made man in the fullest sense, for he had created his own personality and given himself a name to go with it. He was also a rich man, because Conrad invested his money and was a very, very good judge of investments.

He kept on working because he was a restless man, one who would put up with the misery and discomfort of a job like this one rather than vegetate—and because, like his partner, he liked money. There was a healthy streak of greed in both men. They quarreled so bitterly over Hewitt's expense accounts that he spent as little time as possible in Cheyenne.

Conrad dressed like a dandy and lately had taken to wearing a beard. Every time Hewitt saw him he had it trimmed differently. Once he had even tried a monocle. He loved music and played the violin and was learning the piano. He belonged to a literary club and a debating society and, being a single man, was the welcome escort of the prettiest women wherever he went.

Hewitt had seen him last in St. Louis, where they had to testify in the trial of an embezzler. Conrad went out one night—to a concert—with one of the most beautiful women Hewitt had ever seen. What was more to the point, he put her in a hansom cab with flustered haste to get out of introducing Hewitt to her.

"Who was the beauty you were with last night?" Hewitt asked him the next morning.

"That is my personal business," Conrad replied coldly.

"Granted," said Hewitt, "but tell her to get a friend as beautiful as herself, and the four of us will go somewhere every evening."

When he became angry or nervous, Conrad's German accent became more pronounced. "I vould not introduce you to a decent voman, Chefferson," he said. "You are a tomcat, a beast of prey, who puts his vomen on de expense account and den lies about it. You are not to be trusted with a decent voman!"

"Is this one decent? Ah, Conrad, look me in the eye! What happened to your taste for indecent ones?"

"Dog! Bastard! Vy do you make me so mad? How could Gott giff me zuch a bartner as you?"

They were the best of friends.

∿∿∿∿∿

The brakeman moaned and stirred. In a moment Hewitt was able to help him sit up and look around, and in another to remember where he was, why he was there, and what had happened earlier.

"That dirty sonofabitch," he said between his teeth, rubbing his sore jaw. He was almost in tears. "I told him my mother is dying and I've got to get to Seattle, and so he treats me like a slave because I've got to stick with his damn train."

"Take it easy," Hewitt soothed him. "Get your head clear, and then I'm going to show you how to set yourself in with him good."

"I've got to get to Seattle or I'd kill him."

In a few minutes Hewitt glanced at his watch. "How far are we from Pekay Junction?" he asked.

The boomer looked at his own watch. "If I remember the timecard, it's about twenty miles."

"All right," said Hewitt, "here's what we'll do. I'll go down now and eat, and leave you up here. Count six cars ahead. See that bouncer?"

"Yes, an empty, but it's riding pretty good."

"That's not the point. Every now and then there's a little smoke coming from it. Not a hot box. Just some hoboes riding in it, and they've built themselves a little fire on the floor to keep warm. Now, just as we're ready to pull into Pekay Junction, you discover the smoke and tell the Old Man about it. He'll love you if he can find a couple of bindle-stiffs that he can bounce around and throw off out in the middle of nowhere."

"By God, you're right," the boomer whispered. "I saw some smoke there. This is darn nice of you. You could tell the Old Man yourself and get him off your own tail."

"That's right where I want him," Hewitt said, rising to descend the ladder. "I may have to teach him some manners while we're in the junction, watering up. You stay out of it. It's personal."

CHAPTER TWO

When Hewitt descended to the floor of the warm caboose, the burly conductor was just dipping up a bowl of stew. "That worthless bastard able to keep an eye on things?" he growled.

"He's all right," Hewitt said.

"You sure?"

"If I were not, I would not have come down."

"I don't want no halfwit that's half asleep watching my tops."

Hewitt said, "Look, my pot-gutted friend, if you want to make an enemy of me, you're going at it the right way. You may be big, but I've stomped the hell out of a lot of bigger men than you, and if you want to leave this goddamn train stranded out here on the prairie with no crew at all, it's all right with me."

The only other occupant of the caboose was a wireman, a repair and maintenance man for the Great Northern's company telegraph line, which used the same poles as Western Union. He looked well able to take care of himself, but this was not his fight and he was keeping out of it. He lay on one of the long benches and pretended to sleep, his hat over his face, his big canvas bag of tools safely stowed out of the way near the door at the rear of the caboose.

There was no front-end brakeman at all. Many a train had made this run with only a conductor and two brakies —longer trains than this one. But not in weather like this, Hewitt thought, and not with a conductor who was secretly terrified of responsibility.

He helped himself to stew and to a tin cup full of black coffee. He ate a lot, and he ate quickly, knowing that Pekay Junction would be coming up soon. Now and then he glanced up into the cupola and saw the man up there moving about. That was all he needed to know—that he could do his part.

Time passed.

Suddenly the man in the cupola came down the ladder so fast he hit the floor with a thump.

"Hey, skipper," he said, before the conductor could start yelling at him, "six cars ahead there's an empty, and some smoke coming from it. Looks to me like some 'bos in there have built themselves a fire."

The conductor began cursing and slammed down his bowl and spoon. He stood at least six foot three and must have weighed 240. Hewitt thought he had been on a big binge recently, judging by his red-rimmed eyes and the haggard look on his bloated face.

But he could scramble up the ladder fast enough, and scramble right down again, too. Just then the locomotive whistle sounded the signal for a station stop. The conductor ran to his desk and took the .45 out of it.

"You go up to the engine and help fill the tank, London," he said, "and me and this fella will throw them bums out in the snow."

"I'm not handling any tank spouts," Hewitt said. "Let the engine crew do it."

"Goddamm it!" the conductor roared. "Are you gonna take orders or ain't you?"

"No," said Hewitt. "If I wanted to get wet filling the tender tank, I'd be a fireman."

He went on eating. The conductor choked on his own rage for a moment. Then he pointed at the man he had smashed in the jaw.

"Go help water up so we can get the hell out of here," he said.

"All right, skipper."

"I'll help you roust the bindle-stiffs," Hewitt said.

"I don't need no help for that."

"I'll help you anyway."

The train began rattling to a stop as the engineer applied the brakes and the slack went out of the couplers. The wireman was so still he might really have been asleep. It was highly unlikely, Hewitt knew, but the man was not going to be drafted for the nasty job of helping to water the engine or rousting one or more hoboes out of a boxcar.

The boomer opened the front door of the caboose, closed it behind him, and stood on the steps to drop off the moment the train was moving slowly enough for it to be safe. He hit the ground and began running toward the engine to lend a hand. The conductor shoved the big .45 into the pocket of his coat and followed him. Hewitt headed for the rear door.

He slid it open and glanced back at the wireman. His head was still covered by his hat. Hewitt picked up the wireman's heavy canvas bag of tools and set it out on the rear platform. He watched for a moment but the wireman did not move.

Hewitt closed the door and stepped down on the rear stairs, pulling the canvas tool bag over on the rear platform with him. His own two small bags—the luggage to which the conductor had objected—went with it. The water tower was nestled in the center of acres of wood-fenced cattle yard. There were six loading chutes there, so a cattle train could be filled with a minimum loss of time. In the fall of the year this would be a busy spot.

Now it was desolation. There was a section house for the section boss, some bunkhouses for his crew and the pumpman on the water tower, and—nothing else. Just before the train creaked to a stop, Hewitt saw a tall, dense thicket of brush growing near the tracks. The conductor was looking forward eagerly, awaiting a pleasant roust of the unlucky hoboes in the empty boxcar.

Hewitt seized the wireman's tool bag and swung it through the air and into the brush. His own two bags followed. Then he dropped off and ran forward with the conductor.

He could smell the smoke as they neared the car. Far ahead, the boomer with the sore jaw was trotting to catch up with the engine and help handle the big waterspout. The conductor heard Hewitt behind him and turned.

"I told you," he said, "I don't need no help with this. No goddamn hoboes ride my train, and if they try to I take care of it myself."

"Suit yourself," Hewitt said. "You don't mind if I watch, do you?"

At the sliding door of the car, the conductor stopped and took out his .45. He grinned a mean little grin at Hewitt as he braced his feet and put his big left hand against the door.

He gave a lunge, and the door shot back along its rusty

tracks with a grating shriek. Sometimes hoboes were armed, and some of them were dangerous men. The conductor did not expose himself at the door, but he let whoever was inside see his gun.

"Get the hell outa there on the double or you're dead men!" he shouted. "Every damn one of you—out, out, out!"

A second or two of silence, and then a voice quavered, "There's just us two, and you don't need to point that thing around. We're a-comin'."

A gangling man—boy, rather, since he could not be more than twenty-two—appeared in the doorway, hands held high. He had on a warm stocking cap and other clothing to go with it, but he was dirty and unkempt and unhappy-looking.

"Jump," the conductor said.

The kid jumped. The second man appeared. One glance showed that he might have seen better days—he might have been fifty. He wore an overcoat with a worn velvet collar, a felt hat that had once cost good money, and striped pants that looked like part of a suit. His once-fine gaiters were wrecked now, his big toe peeping through the left one.

"I can't jump that. At my age, and as weak as I am from hunger, I'd break something. You might as well shoot me," he said in a quiet voice.

The conductor raised the revolver. He cocked it slowly, so the double click was audible.

"Jump," was all he said.

Hewitt reached under his coat and took out his own gun. He took two quick steps forward and shoved its muzzle into the conductor's back.

"If you care to look around," he said, "you'll see another

forty-five, but make one motion I don't like and it's the last thing you'll ever see. Now let that hammer down slowly—and keep that damn thing pointed to the ground."

"You sonofabitch," the conductor said softly.

But he did as he was told. Hewitt reached down and took the .45 from him with his left hand and thrust it into his own coat pocket.

"Now go help the man down," he said.

"I'll see you and him both in hell first!" the conductor shouted, spinning on his heel.

Hewitt stepped back, keeping his gun aimed at the conductor's big gut. "That can be arranged," he said, "if that's what you want. But first you're going to help that man down."

He waited. So did the conductor. So did the shabby man in the door of the boxcar. Then the conductor turned again in defeat. He put up his hand. The shabbily well-dressed hobo leaned over and took hold of it. The conductor's enormous strength supported him lightly and easily to the ground.

Hewitt gestured with the .45 to the two hoboes. "Over there, out of the way," he said. "About twenty feet will be right. And the first one of you to make a move—count on it, I'll drill you."

Suddenly he put both his .45 and the conductor's in the door of the empty boxcar and pushed them back out of the way.

"You were so free with your fists with that fellow you sent up to help fill the tank," he said to the conductor, "and you've got such a big mouth, I think it's time you got a lesson. Here's where you and I part company, but by God you're going to remember me for a long, long time."

The huge conductor could not believe his luck. He jumped at Hewitt with both fists pumping. He had fought many a man in the prize ring before he went to pieces—Hewitt saw that too late, and knew he was up against a heavyweight, a pro.

All he could do was cover up and retreat and take most of it on his shoulders and the top of his head. He took a left hook to his right ribs, too, and went breathless as pain shot through his whole body. He risked two quick left jabs at the gut and landed both, but hurting this beast was not enough. You had to hurt him again and again and again.

Hewitt took another left hook that was agony. It straightened him up and dropped his arms, but instead of coming in for the kill, the big conductor stepped back and reached into his pocket. His right hand came out glittering with heavy brass knucks.

"You smart little sonofabitch," he said, "you're going to ache all the way to the division point and you're going to work your ass off every minute of the way, and when we get there—oh, man, will I put you out of commission for a month!"

A man who stood and made a speech while he had you paralyzed was a cocksure fool. Hewitt got his breath and his hand went to his shirt pocket. He let the big beast come at him, his metal-knuckled right fist cocked.

Hewitt jumped and came inside the fist with the knucks, swinging the sap and snapping his wrist with both skill and vindictive force. The sap landed smartly on the forehead. The conductor made not a sound as his arms came down and his legs went limp. He collapsed on his face in the snow in an inert heap.

Hewitt retrieved both guns. Neither hobo had moved. He put the conductor's gun in his pocket but held his own in his right hand.

"Good thinking, boys," he said. "We've got only one chance to get out of here, and it's not the train. Come on and load this slab of meat in the caboose."

The two had to grunt and strain to lift the unconscious conductor, but Hewitt kept the gun on them and did not offer to help. Even after they had carried him back and piled him on the back platform of the caboose, he did not move.

The engine tanks had been filled with water and the engineer blew his whistle for a signal. None came, the conductor being still unconscious. Soon the brakeman came trotting down along the train.

The conductor was just beginning to stir. Hewitt stripped him of his brass knucks and pocketed them.

"You two are going to have to get this train the rest of the way," he said to the brakeman. He reached over and shook the moaning, twitching conductor. "You!" he said sharply. "Wake up. Rise and shine! Get down to the yard office—you've got to take the Flyer out in twenty minutes."

"Flyer? Flyer?" For a moment the conductor thought it was the callboy at the division point. He sat up blearily. "Whatcha mean, Flyer? Where are we? Who the hell are you?"

It took the dazed conductor a few minutes to understand that he now had only one brakeman, and that it would be wise to try to get along with him in the future.

He had to be helped into the caboose, and it was the brakeman who gave the engineer the highball.

"I dunno what happened, London," the brakeman said from the rear platform as the train began to move, "and I don't think I want to. So long . . . and thanks."

~~~~~~

The train was no sooner out of sight than a rider on an excellent horse appeared beyond the wooden cattle pens. Hewitt holstered his gun and waited for him. It was a big, lanky, gray-haired man with a strong, stern face, but he slid from the saddle like a lithe boy to grasp Hewitt's hand.

"Jeff! By the Lord, it's good to see you, but I thought you never would get here," he said.

"I was delayed," Jeff replied, "but I knew I could count on you. Got a good horse for me?"

"Now, would I have any other kind?"

"I don't suppose you could find a couple more, with saddles and bridles? I've got a couple of friends here who might want to go along with me."

The old man scratched his face gravely. "Why," he said, "I reckon I could scratch up a couple, if it's important."

Jeff looked at the two hoboes. "I'm heading for Canada by a private trail of mine. Does that sound good to you?"

"Canada?" cried the older of the two hoboes. "What part?"

"Well," said Hewitt, "I could say Regina and then Prince Albert, but I won't. But it'll be in that general direction."

"Anywhere near the Casewell ranch?"

"Never heard of it."

"It's the Big C Little c brand," the hobo said eagerly. "Everybody knows it. Just a little north of Regina but south of the Qu'Appelle."

"Last time I was through there, Sir Philip Quarles owned the Big C Little c."

"Yes, but he sold it to Jim Casewell. That's exactly where I'd like to go, and I may say I'll reward you handsomely when we get there."

Hewitt looked at the younger hobo. "How about you— are you Canada-bound?"

"One place is as good as another to me," said the youth.

"Then we may as well get acquainted. Jeff Hewitt's the name," Hewitt said, offering his hand.

Bill Denny was the young man. The rundown, older man was Arthur C. Peck—or so he said. Hewitt left them waiting by the tracks while he walked with the other man, leading the fine horse through the acres of cattle pens.

"Hate to put you to all this trouble," said Hewitt, "but I was up against it, Pete."

"You know it's no trouble to do somethin' for you," said Pete Kinsey, owner of the PK ranch, which was the only outfit served by what the Northern Pacific called Pekay Junction. "When you helped me out of that jam, I told you to call on me for anything, and I meant it."

"You paid me for that and I'll pay you for this."

Kinsey grinned from the side of his mouth. He was another tough one, a rowdy and a troublemaker and a gunman in his youth, who had gone respectable after getting married. Hewitt had introduced him to his wife. She was

the one person on earth who could cow Kinsey and make
him like it.

"I ain't goin' to ask what you're doin'," said Kinsey,
"but I'd bet a dime to a doughnut it's the old guy with the
overcoat."

"You'd win that," said Hewitt.

"Who's the kid?"

"I don't know. Just some drifter that Peck attached
himself to because he's helpless alone. Pete, I've followed
that scalawag for over a month. I've slept in bedbuggy
hotels and in hobo camps and God knows where all, to
keep him in sight. And I just proved one thing."

"What's that?"

"That he's Canada-bound. And all that means is that
now the real job begins."

"Sometimes," Kinsey said wistfully, "I'd like to get out
and kick up my heels the way you do, but I reckon I'm a
tame grizzly now. Here's the horses, and I brought plenty
of saddle grub."

"I knew I could count on you. How much do I owe you,
Pete?"

"Just get my horses back, is all."

"That's the one thing I can't promise. How much have
you got tied up in this outfit?"

Kinsey scratched his chin. "Oh—say three hundred fifty
for horses, saddles, bridles, and grub."

"You lie like a book agent." Hewitt took a small note-
book from his pocket and scribbled a few lines on it.
"Send this to my partner. He'll mail you a draft for five
hundred. It'll come out of an expense account so rich you
can buy Mrs. Kinsey something pretty with a clear conscience."

Kinsey stuffed the paper in his pocket without looking

at it. "Sure wish I was goin' with you," he said, "but I'm a sober old cowman now."

"And a lucky one."

"Jeff, I never knowed you to make a mistake before, but if I's you, the first thing I'd do after I get to Canada is check in with the North-West Mounted Police. They're tetchy."

"I've had that in mind. This is one I can't afford to make a mistake on. I've chased this Peck too far."

~~~~~~

From the generous supplies Kinsey had brought them, they took time to boil coffee, fry bacon, and bake some biscuits before leaving. The last thing Hewitt did was drag the wireman's canvas kit out of the brush.

"Either of you know how to send or receive Morse code?" he asked.

Neither did. He opened the kit and buckled on the wireman's climbing spurs and belt. He took out a test set, climbed the pole, and clipped it to the Western Union line. He was not the fastest man in the world on the wires, but he was accurate and he could talk the language of the telegraphers along the line and get them to take a relay. His wire said:

COLLECT URGENT DAY RATES:

CONRAD MEUSE
BANKERS BONDING AND INDEMNITY CO
CHEYENNE WYO
USING JH NORTHBOUND QUARLES WIRE ME

PATTERSON REGINA IF OTHER PAPER TURNED
UP ELSEWHERE STOP NEED KNOW ABOUT BEARERS
STOP IF THEY APPEAR ELSEWHERE WE HAVE
CANADIAN F PLUS E

He felt sure that Conrad would have the telegram before the night was far advanced, if not before dusk. They used the wires extensively, for although it was expensive, sometimes time was dearer still.

From this cryptic message Conrad would learn that Hewitt would be using his own name, that he would be found eventually at the Big C Little c, and that he would see Franklyn Patterson, a banker, when he passed through Regina. Also, that he hoped by the time he got there Conrad could report on whether sixty thousand dollars' worth of bearer bonds had turned up anywhere else.

If they had not, then whoever had bought the Big C Little c from Sir Philip Quarles had forged someone's name to some ordinary registered bonds, and they would have a Canadian forgery case as well as a New York embezzlement.

The snow had stopped and a warmish breeze was blowing softly. It made him feel good as he came down the pole. What made him feel still better was that the case in which he was having so much fine sport involved a missing $275,500. Conrad had negotiated a straight thirty per cent on all the bearer bonds recovered, fifteen per cent on the others, and ten thousand dollars each for arrest and conviction of the embezzlers. Fun was fun; on the other hand, there was nothing quite like money.

He strapped his two bags on behind the saddle of the best of the three horses. "Let's ride," he said.

CHAPTER THREE

The tardy spring of Saskatchewan had come by the time they crossed the border two weeks later, having taken their time.

It could not be said that any memorable friendship had sprung up, but they had worked out a good form of teamwork that made travel easy. Denny and Peck were both penniless. Both tried to thank Hewitt for paying their way.

"Drop it," he said. "You'd do it for me. Working stiffs have to stick together."

"I suppose so," said Arthur C. Peck, "but I'm afraid that by your standards, sir, I have never qualified as a working stiff."

"Oh?"

Peck smiled a wan and sheepish smile. "Oh indeed. I don't ask you to believe it, but I've spent exactly forty years in finance—stocks and bonds. Started as an office boy at the age of twelve in a broker's office when there were not more than a hundred real brokers in New York. Got out of the business the hard way last October, and I'll be fifty-three in July."

He seemed to want to talk about it. "The hard way? What's that?" Hewitt asked.

"Two firms I worked for earlier in my career went

broke," said Peck. "I could always get a job because it
was well known that they went broke because they had
disregarded my advice. An enviable reputation, that's
what I had in those days."

"And now?"

"For all I know," said Peck, "I'm a fugitive from justice.
My last firm, in which I was a junior partner, went broke
last fall. I was in Boston for a couple of days. When I returned to New York, I went down to the office late one
morning and I found it closed. A small crowd of clients
and customers had collected in the doorway. I'm sure it's
unnecessary to say that there was an element of hostility
in the way they greeted me."

Hewitt grinned. The seedy little man had a sort of
trampish gallantry about him, whether you could believe
all of what he said or not.

"What happened?"

"I sent for a policeman, who sent for other policemen,
who sent for prosecutors and auditors and all the funereal
functionaries of bankruptcy. We used my key to enter.

"To make a long story short but no less dreary, my two
partners had skipped out with everything they could lay
their hands on. It was quite a bit, I may say. It shook the
hell out of the market for nearly two weeks. Ah, me!"

Peck looked about, seeing the miles and miles of fresh,
green prairie dotted with tiny touches of color where
early spring flowers were starting to bloom. Plainly, all
this beauty saddened him and took his mind back to his
tragedy in New York with more pain than ever.

"Fortunately," he went on after a moment, "I had antici-
pated some slippage and had gone heavily short with
every cent I had. I signed over my accounts to the

receiver the judge put in charge. Stocks I had bought on ten-per-cent margin had slipped more than that. One hell of a lot more!"

"I should think," said Hewitt, "that turning your winnings over to them voluntarily would have been much in your favor. When you go flat broke to make up for someone else's embezzlement—"

"Oh," Peck cut in, "it helped, of course, at first. Over a hundred fifty thousand dollars, and I don't call that small change, sir."

"Neither do I. Why did you skip, then?"

"Because," Peck said with a rueful smile, "the suspicious scoundrels began wondering why I had sold short. You see, I did not sell through our own office. I went to another broker. The question naturally arose—did I know my partners were looting us and was I trying to cash in?"

"I can see how they might think that," said Hewitt, "but surely you could prove otherwise."

"Unfortunately, I couldn't. I had had my suspicions of my partners and had taken certain steps to warn a few customers who were personal friends that I didn't like the look of certain things. Unfortunately, even friends sometimes talk too much."

"That they do."

"One friend, truer than the others, tipped me that a warrant had been issued and that officers of the court were waiting at my house to arrest me. I couldn't even slip in to pack a suitcase, and I couldn't cash a check. I had enough cash for a ticket to Pittsburgh."

"Why Pittsburgh?"

"Who goes to Pittsburgh? Only people who have to. I had the reputation of a man of taste, sir, and I thought they would be looking for me in such cultural centers as Boston, Washington, London, Paris, or Berlin. After Pittsburgh I went to Minneapolis. Ah, me! If anyone had told me, a year ago that I would be riding a horse across the Saskatchewan prairie, looking forward to beans fried over a campfire for supper, I would have called him a lunatic."

"We never know, do we?" said Hewitt. He looked at the younger man, Bill Denny. "What's your story?"

"Well," said Denny, "I sure never left no hundred fifty thousand dollars behind."

He was twenty-four years old and had been manager of a small but profitable cattle ranch in Colorado. He was successful beyond his wildest dreams at age twenty-two, with a steady job, a good house to live in, and a wife he adored.

"Neither one of us knowed it," he said, "but she had the consumption when we was married. It took her nigh onto eight months to die. Eight months! I let the work go to hell to be with her. I had me a good bunch of men, and they didn't need no drivin' to keep things up.

"Only, after she died, I just couldn't stand it there no longer. Besides, the doctor said I might have took a touch of TB myself from taking care of her and ought to go live outdoors and never see the inside of a house for a year, until I knowed for sure. I know now that I ain't got the consumption. But I don't know if I'm glad about it or not."

"What was her name?" Hewitt asked.

"Cherry. Not short for Charity—there was a cherry tree blooming outside the window when she was born. She—she was the *best* wife—!"

He choked up, and for a long time the three rode in silence. It was broken by Peck.

"Somehow," he said to Hewitt, "you look familiar to me. I wonder, have I known you sometime in the past?"

"I don't remember it," Hewitt said quite truthfully. "But I've been in New York quite a bit, so you may have seen me."

"You're a college man, aren't you?"

"Nope."

"You talk like one. Odd to think back and recall that you were a mere boomer brakeman, and now to see how competent you are on a horse, and—"

"My friend," Hewitt interrupted him, "I've done a lot of jobs in my time and learned a little bit on every one. Usually managed to enjoy life, too."

"I can't imagine what pleasure there would be in working for that brute of a conductor."

"You can't? The way I quit that job gave me more pleasure than anything I've done in years."

"I see."

Bill Denny said, a little shyly, "Seems to me I seen you in Minneapolis, when I was hangin' around there, before me and Mr. Peck throwed in together. Only you was pretty well dressed then, seems like. I kind of remember you coming out of a big restaurant when I was standin' there with an empty gut and not a dime in my pocket."

"I wouldn't be surprised," Hewitt said. "I was in Minneapolis for quite a while, and I like to dress well and eat in the best places when I'm in funds. But, in my small way, I have an even sadder story than our friend Peck."

"Impossible," Peck said.

"Ever play poker?"

"Oh, of course."

"Well enough to know when it's an honest game against good players, not a crook in the crowd?"

"I may not be that expert, but I know enough to get up and leave a game when I sense something wrong."

"There was nothing wrong with this game. I can show you ways to deal cards that would make you swear off the game of poker forever, but this was with five good men and true. A hand of stud, and I was dealing it myself."

He was lying now and enjoying it. So were Peck and Denny. Everybody liked poker stories.

"I'd won a few hundred and I had two thousand in my money belt. First card I dealt myself was a king. My down card was the ace of spades. I drew a king of hearts up, so I bet twenty. Everybody stayed, and damned if I didn't deal myself another ace.

"One fellow had a pair of eights showing, so it was his bet. He shoved in fifty. Another fellow had two hearts showing. He stayed. So did I. Everybody else dropped out.

"Fourth card I dealt the fellow with the eights drew a jack of clubs and the other fellow drew another heart. I drew the king of hearts. Here I am with two big pairs, and a man who's trying to build a flush, but I've already got his king. That cuts the odds a little.

"Fellow with the pair shoved in a couple of hundred. We both stayed. I dealt him a five of spades and the other fellow another heart. My downfall was that I dealt myself the ten of hearts."

He had them breathless with anticipation now.

"Fellow with the pair of eights showing turned over his

hand and showed another jack. 'Two pairs,' he said, 'and my hunch is they ain't good enough.' So, I was still high man and I had another heart that the other fellow needed for his flush."

"That cuts the odds against a flush so much," Denny cut in quietly, "and I can see how a man would be led on. You with two big pairs, kings and aces—Goddlemighty! Only, I bet he had the other heart on you, didn't he?"

"And all my money before I checked it to him. That's why you see me booming my way along Jim Hill's main line, cheerfully quitting my job at the right moment."

A sigh from Arthur C. Peck. "I can see how you might be in the mood to enjoy whipping that conductor."

Hewitt laughed. "I guess he paid a good part of the bill for that fifth heart. I had spotted you fellows' smoke long before I said anything. So long as you didn't set the car on fire, I wanted to wait until we hit that junction where I had a friend."

"I thought that was exceedingly lucky."

"Not lucky. It has been my habit to make my own luck wherever possible, by picking time, place, and circumstances."

"Partners too, I'm sure."

"Mr. Peck, I'm an unsociable cuss and I don't often go partners with anybody. I have to see a man in Regina and I'll be there a few days before heading north on business that I don't care to discuss. You two want to ride along— fine! I've got money enough to get us to Regina and I'll get more there.

"But I'm not talking partners. Somebody to ride and camp with is mighty fine, but that's as far as it goes."

"How about these horses?" Denny asked. "Seems to me that man Kinsey must be a mighty good friend to mount all three of us this well."

"He is."

"What do we do with the horses?"

"I'll tell you when the time comes. I'd tell you now if I knew."

They rode in silence for a few minutes. Then Peck said, "Mr. Hewitt, all my life I tried to run an honest business among scamps. I did not succeed, but I learned a little about human nature."

"Yes?"

"Yes. And frankly, I'm not sure I believe a damn word you've told us."

Hewitt laughed heartily. "You just go on feeling that way about strangers and you'll probably never be taken in by crooked partners again."

Peck nodded. "I'm sure you're right," he said, "but it's a hell of a thing, at the age of fifty-two, to discover that it's unwise to trust anybody on earth, even the man who befriended us as you did."

"That's life," said Hewitt.

For a while it was just a dim blot on the northern horizon, but Hewitt and Denny knew that it was a clump of trees and trees meant a creek. They reached it just before dark, and no pleasanter camping ground could have been imagined. During the last two hours Hewitt had amused himself and awed his two companions by carrying his .45 in his hand, cocked, to fire at prairie chickens.

He emptied the gun—six shots—and brought down six prairie chickens. They built a fire under the birch and alder trees, skinned and roasted the chickens, and then Hewitt got out his declining stock of excellent cigars. They sat smoking and talking desultorily far into the night.

Night made Peck morose, reminding him of how far he had fallen from his days as a stockbroker. It made Denny a little less withdrawn, as though companionship made the pain of his widowerhood a little easier to bear. It made Hewitt eagerly if quietly optimistic.

Manhunting was not always fun. Often it was hard, brutal work, and sometimes it required decisions and moral judgments that were painful to make. Lost trails drove Hewitt crazy. Tonight he was enjoying a rest during a long, easy, pleasant ride, the decisions and judgments were all made, and he thought he was well on schedule on one of the richest cases he had ever worked.

He slept as close to the fire as he could get, using his saddle as a pillow. Under it he put the .45 he had taken from the Great Northern conductor. He had never been uneasy about these two before, and although he went to sleep instantly, some sort of warning seemed to thrum through his nerves like a lightly plucked, open E string of a good fiddle.

When he woke he did so without moving or changing his breathing. He supposed he had been asleep no more than an hour. He could hear nothing, see nothing, smell nothing.

But just then he felt a slight shifting of the saddle that

was his pillow. He snatched the sap out of his hip pocket as he rolled over and launched himself through the air.

He landed on top of Arthur C. Peck and found himself staring down into the muzzle of the conductor's .45.

"Put it down," he said, brandishing the sap, "or I'll be forced to beat your brains out."

Denny came awake and sat up, but he did not interfere.

"On the other hand," Peck said calmly, "I could pull the trigger and blow your brains out instead."

"You could if the gun was loaded."

"Oh, well!" Peck tossed the gun aside. "I have made another miscalculation, haven't I? As you see, I'm not familiar with firearms."

Hewitt thrust the gun back under the saddle. "I am," he said.

"I hope this isn't going to make any difference in our relationship," Peck said, getting up and dusting himself off.

Hewitt said nothing. He laid a few more pieces of dead wood on the fire and curled up to sleep again.

"Mr. Peck," said Bill Denny, "why in the hell did you do it?"

"Take the gun, you mean? Or try to take it? Oh, I just thought I should like to have an ace in the hole myself when I'm sitting in a game with Mr. Hewitt."

"That ain't the way to do it, I can tell you that."

"I can see that now," Peck said. He lay down again, turned up the worn velvet collar of his coat to cover his neck, and was instantly asleep. The last thing Hewitt heard was Denny's soft, wondering exclamation: "Sonofa-*bitch*, if they ain't a pair!"

CHAPTER FOUR

Almost the moment you crossed the Canadian border you became aware of a frontier atmosphere that was wilder, freer, and in some ways tougher than the one you had left behind. For one thing, some of the Indian tribes consigned to reservations by the United States had refused to go, and instead had fled to Canada, where they were welcomed. There was room there for them to keep to themselves and live in friendship with the native Canadians and the Canadian settlers.

But the Indians still bore a grudge against Americans, and Indian families on peaceful rides to visit relatives could turn into miniature war parties if they ran into isolated Americans.

The North West Territories were filling rapidly, and agitation for the formation of provinces and self-government was growing. A newer country than western America was in birth, and it was big—big and empty despite the homesteaders and the trainloads of new settlers who arrived almost weekly.

Regina was a tough town, but not as tough as it might have been because the headquarters of the North-West Mounted Police was there. This elite force, more like the Texas Rangers than any other police organization, had already achieved a reputation for integrity, toughness, determination, and endless patience.

In Regina, Hewitt bought supplies, some cooking utensils, and a half-wild pony. They made camp outside of town, and he left young Bill Denny to break the pony to work as a packhorse. He had grown to like the young man who was a born outdoorsman, a lot.

"You help him in any way you can," he told Peck, "but don't get yourself hurt. I'm heading north as soon as I've got a packhorse, and I'm not waiting for any cripples to get well."

"I shall take every precaution," said Peck. "As you have seen, I'm barely able to stay in the saddle on a tame horse. About the only thing I can do to assist Bill is stand aside and make faces at the horse when he needs to feel our displeasure."

"Bill will tell you what to do."

"May one ask what you will be doing, sir?"

"One may. I have some private business of my own to transact, and I mean to keep it private."

Peck sighed. "I can take a hint. May one also inquire about the possibility of a loan to get warmer and more-fitting clothing before we head north?"

"Mr. Peck," said Hewitt, "we'll see that you both get clothes, but you don't want them too warm. Saskatchewan's cold in the winter, but the summers can be hotter than hell, and the first warm weather will bring out the deer flies and mosquitoes. If you plan on being here very long, you'll want to sleep under mosquito netting instead of heavy blankets."

Peck looked disappointed. Daily he had grown shabbier, but the first morning they were together Hewitt had gotten out his razor and shaved, and then let the other two shave. Now Hewitt and Peck shaved daily, while young Bill Denny shaved once a week.

Peck also washed out his one shirt whenever he had the time to let it dry, but of his other clothing, only his overcoat remained serviceable. His black suit was in rags and his gaiters were falling to pieces. His generally disreputable appearance was not really helped much by a clean-shaven face. He looked exactly like what Hewitt thought he was—not much more than a confidence man who had fallen on hard times.

Hewitt left them struggling with the wild pony and rode to the Volney Private Bank, Ltd., in Regina. It was a solid-looking stone cube of a building.

He went inside and immediately felt like he was in London. All the rest of Canada might be wild, vital, vigorous, noisy, and slightly uncouth at times, but Volney Private Bank, Ltd., with branches all over the world, was a touch of London everywhere. He presented himself at the desk of an old man with long gray hair, who was working at a thick ledger, his glasses on the end of his nose.

"May I see Mr. Franklyn Patterson?" Hewitt asked.

The old man looked up condescendingly. "May I ask the reason for wishing to see Mr. Patterson?"

Hewitt took out his wallet and put down one of his Bankers Bonding and Indemnity Company cards. "I think he will be expecting me," he said.

The old clerk looked at the card and then at Hewitt's rough clothing and again at the card. "*You* are Mr. Jefferson Hewitt?" he said.

Hewitt did not bother to reply. The old man got up,

took off his green eyeshade, smoothed his hair, and marched to a closed door in the rear of the bank. He rapped gently on it and then vanished inside. In a moment he came out again.

"If you will come this way, sir," he said.

Hewitt went into the manager's office of the bank. Behind the desk sat a big, florid-looking man with piercing blue eyes and a tremendous blond mustache. He stood up slowly, frowning as he put out his hand and gave Hewitt a strong grip.

"Not everyone could be presumed to know that I am expecting a partner of BB and I," he said, "so I'm sure you're Mr. Hewitt. But I am required by my instructions to secure some identification from you."

Hewitt stood up straight, hands at his sides, a rather vacant, idiotic look on his face, and recited:

> *"The shades of night were falling fast,*
> *As through an Alpine village passed*
> *A youth, who bore, 'mid snow and ice,*
> *A banner with the strange device—*
> *Excelsior!"*

The banker gaped at him. "Go on," he said.

"That is the first of nine verses of one of Henry Wadsworth Longfellow's least successful poems," he said. "My partner, Mr. Meuse, is a cautious man, and sometimes he carries it to extremes."

"Very well, I have to take you at your word," said Franklyn Patterson. "How the devil am I supposed to secure a copy of Wadsworth's poems, or whatever his name was, out here? I was barely able to identify him through the local schoolmaster."

"I give you my word," Hewitt said, laughing, "that this is far from being the most ridiculous code signal Conrad has ever used."

"Conrad who?"

"Conrad Meuse."

The banker seemed completely satisfied. "I have a telegraphic draft for five thousand American dollars, which I can pay you at any time," he said. "I also have this telegram addressed to you, and I may say it has caused me no little curiosity. I know of your company, of course, but we have never done business with you and wondered what would bring you here."

"I'll tell you about that in a minute," said Hewitt. He opened the telegram from Conrad Meuse and read:

NO SIGN ANY PAPER ANYWHERE STOP ONE MISSING
PARTNER W. O. BREWER MURDERED BY GARROTING
DETROIT POSID STOP ROBINOT JOINING YOU STOP
BEAR DOWN LOSS INCREASING DAILY AUDIT

As accustomed as he was to reading Conrad's codes, he had to frown over this one. "Posid," of course, meant "positive identification"; so he could take it for granted that one William Oscar Brewer was dead. "Robinot" must mean Robinson of Ottawa, since he remembered a private investigator in Ottawa by the name of Robinson. They had worked together on an international case and Hewitt remembered him as a big, clumsy, stubborn, opinionated cockney, formerly a London bobby. He was a plodder who did detail work well but had no trace of imagination. He might come in handy—so long as he stayed in Ottawa.

He folded the telegram and put it in his pocket. "I'll want some dollars and pounds—say, one thousand dollars and five hundred pounds," he said. "I suppose the pound is easier to circulate."

"In fewer and fewer areas, I'm afraid," replied Patterson. "We're Americanizing rapidly because Ottawa won't give us provincial government, and I'm not sure which side I'm on."

"May I ask if you have ever heard of a three-partner brokerage house by the name of Carlton, Brewer and Peck?"

"Who hasn't? They went smash with half a million of clients' money and vanished. My God, don't tell me your firm had them bonded!"

Hewitt smiled. "No, but when others make similar mistakes, we're often called upon to correct them, which is why I'm here. I wonder, do you happen to know Sir Philip Quarles or the man to whom he sold his ranch?"

"Sir Philip and I are old friends. I met the other chap once. A Mr. Vincent McCarthy, an American."

"What does he look like?"

"Why, as I remember, he's about your size, very black hair, blue eyes. All business—damned rude, in fact!"

"I suppose Sir Philip returned to England when he sold out?"

"He was going to, I know that, and took passage with Lady Quarles on the railway for the East. He has a home here in Regina and he put it up for sale, too. Curious thing, though: I had a note from him just this morning, saying he was back but rather incognito, don't you know. He's coming to the house—my house—late tonight to see me about something."

A shiver of anticipation ran through Hewitt. "Is he back in his own house?"

"Why, I had assumed so. But the whole blasted thing had such a conspiratorial air about it, don't you know, that I decided to await him."

"Mr. Patterson," Hewitt said earnestly, "it is of the utmost importance that I see Sir Philip as soon as possible, and I'd like a letter of introduction from you."

"Quite impossible," Patterson said firmly. "Sir Philip indicated that, er, extreme discretion was required."

"He is so right! Let me try to persuade you. I know where Mr. Peck is—Mr. Peck of the firm of Carlton, Brewer and Peck. He has not two pennies to rub together. Mr. Brewer died criminally, at the hands of a garroter, in Detroit. Unknown to me is the whereabouts of Mr. Carlton, whom we may justly suspect of possessing the boodle."

"I'm afraid, sir, that I see no connection."

"In case you don't know it, Mr. Patterson, a man choosing an alias unconsciously imitates his own name in some way. Carlton—McCarthy. I'm afraid that Mr. Carlton, alias Vincent McCarthy, may have victimized Sir Philip, with some of the stolen securities. Why else should Sir Philip return clandestinely to Regina and seek a secret meeting with you?"

"Good God!" The banker turned pale. "Why—why, I've got forty thousand dollars' worth of New York Central construction bonds that I bought at a discount from Mr. McCarthy because he needed cash. And I know that Sir Philip received ten thousand dollars in cash and forty thousand in bonds for his ranch. My God, this—why, this could be a disaster!"

"Have you got your New York Central bonds where you can get at them?"

"They're in the vault. Why?"

"I assume they're not bearer bonds?"

"No, but they're all endorsed before a notary public."

"Mr. Patterson, anyone hawking that much in stolen bonds isn't going to have any pangs of conscience if he steals a notary's seal. Can you give me just the serial numbers and amounts of three of those bonds, so that I can wire to see if they're part of the loot? And then, dammit, let's go see Sir Philip!"

Within an hour they were hurrying along to the railroad station and telegraph office, where Hewitt sent the following wire to Meuse:

VERIFY NYC BONDS ES 505–1183 FIVE THOU STOP
VS 505–069 ONE THOU STOP VS 511–238 ONE THOU
STOP ALL CASPER PUCEK STOP REPLY CARE PATTERSON

〰〰〰〰〰

Sir Philip Quarles was a diminutive man with a shrill voice and the tension of desperation. Formerly he had worn handsomely curled sidewhiskers and London suits; now he had returned clean-shaven, in a cheap suit, and wearing a broad-brimmed cattleman's hat. And instead of opening his house he was living at the Commercial House, the kind of place where Hewitt stayed only when he had to.

Had they seen Sir Philip first, the wire to Conrad would have been unnecessary.

"What damnable, stupid simpletons we are," Sir Philip whimpered. "Moment I got to Ottawa and handed the bonds to my broker, he told me they were stolen. Yet the man is so—so convincing, so plausible! He had to be talked into buying my property. Didn't fancy it, don't you know."

"Describe him, please," said Hewitt.

"Oh—fifty-five years old. Expressionless face, blue eyes, and I believe wears a black toupee. Carries a forty-five, I know that, and once dropped a hint that he was a bit of an expert with it."

"At least you can get your ranch back," said Franklyn Patterson, trying to comfort him.

"Not without a distressing lawsuit that will expose me for a perfect ass," Sir Philip said with a moan. "He turned right around and sold it."

"For cash?"

"Yes, and at a dreadful loss. Paid me seventy-five thousand American and sold it for sixty thousand."

"Must be a hell of a big place."

"An empire!" Patterson exclaimed. "Could run twenty thousand head of cattle there, Mr. Hewitt."

"You got ten thousand in cash, Sir Philip," said Hewitt. "What did you do with it?"

"Once I learned the bonds were stolen," the baronet replied, "I turned over what was left of it—almost eight thousand—to the authorities in Ottawa. It can't be traced, I'm sure."

"It may be possible. Were the bills banded?"

"To be sure."

"Happen to remember if the name of any bank was stamped or imprinted on the bands?"

"Why, I believe Shippers and Mercantile of New York, and—let's see, United States Traders and Factors of Detroit was one."

"Were those bands still on them when you turned them in at Ottawa?"

"Of course not. In my own home I counted those bills one at a time, tied them into one big bale, and put them in a valise that never left my side."

"And the Ottawa authorities didn't ask?"

"No. But, Mr. Hewitt, I retained the services of an excellent private detective to help me. Chap by the name of—"

"I know, Julius A. Robinson."

"My word, you already know that!"

"Yes. What's the name of the man who bought the place from McCarthy—or Carlton, as we all think."

"Ralph Elphinstone. Dreadful thing is, he's an old friend of mine. Married an American girl, years ago, a black girl who slipped through on the Underground Railway. Delightful family, almost all grown now. I—I would almost rather lose the fifty-five thousand dollars than make him bear the loss."

"You may have to anyway," Hewitt said.

CHAPTER FIVE

Regina was a lively town and not as uncouth as many frontier towns Hewitt had visited. All about it, small family groups of Indians were encamped—Assiniboin, Santee, and some who looked like the fierce, proud Ogallalas who had left the United States rather than submit to reservation life.

Here they were assigned reservations too, but they could move about more freely as long as they did not look for trouble, and above all, the laws against selling liquor to them were strictly enforced. The Indians had no experience with alcohol, no knowledge of it, no tribal tradition that dealt with it.

In the United States the penalties for selling alcohol to Indians were severe—on the books. But graft, mismanagement, and above all a calculated policy of using alcohol to help exterminate the troublesome race made the law a farce. The United States Army had fought the Indians too hard and too long not to condone any measure that would reduce them to impotent indigence.

Hewitt, Denny, and Peck spent the rest of the afternoon buying clothing. Hewitt dressed as he always tried to dress—dark cutaway coat, white shirt with dark stock, dark pants stuffed into good cowboy boots, and a wide-brimmed black hat creased like a cavalryman's. He

went into a barber shop for a haircut and shave and to
have his mustache trimmed.

Bill Denny wanted only Levi's and blue hickory shirts,
but he accepted gratefully new boots, socks, underwear,
and a hat. Hewitt also bought him a holster and gave him
the Colt .45 he had taken from the Great Northern conductor.

It was impossible to make Arthur C. Peck look like anything but what he was—a city man mislaid like a lost
penny on the prairie. Hewitt bought him riding breeches,
flat-heeled boots, a peaked outdoor hat like the Mounties
wore except that it was black, and the greenhorn's identi-
fying red-checked coat.

"We'll camp here one more night," Hewitt said, "and
tomorrow I've got one more call to make. Then we'll head
north for a chat with Mr. Elphinstone."

"What do you expect to learn from him?" Peck asked.

"I'm sure I don't know, but you go where the trail leads
you." Hewitt turned to Denny. "Bill, how do you feel
about going along?"

"It don't matter to me where I go," Denny replied, "and
I owe you for saving me a hell of a beating by that conductor."

"You owe me nothing, my friend. I'm sure you can find
a job somewhere around here, and I want you to remember you're free to do so."

"Reckon I'll stick with you. I ain't goin' *to* no place, Mr.
Hewitt. I'm runnin' *from* hell on earth."

They ate in town that night and then returned to camp
among the Indians just outside town. All around they
could see twinkling campfires. They no sooner had their

own going than they saw a rider coming toward them. He pulled up a rod or two away to hail them.

"I say there! I'm coming in to talk with you. Police, don't you know."

"Come right ahead, Constable," said Hewitt. "It may save me a trip."

The young man who rode up to the fire was well mounted and his horse was well equipped, with even a double bit, two pairs of reins, and a surcingle. The man himself was dressed in the handsome dress uniform of the North-West Mounted Police.

"You are Mr. Jefferson Hewitt of Bankers Bonding and Indemnity Company, I presume," he said, with a somewhat adenoidy, upper-class British accent. "I'm Constable Ranald Hewston. Had a dreadful time finding you after I talked to Sir Philip."

"I was coming to see you in the morning," said Hewitt, offering his hand. "A pleasure to know you."

"Charmed. The superintendent and his adjutant were called to Ottawa and the assistant superintendent is off to see about a bit of trouble up around Prince Albert. I hear from Sir Philip that you're a private-inquiry agent on an embezzlement case."

"That's right," said Hewitt, "and I wouldn't be surprised to learn that it's the same case that called your superiors to the capital."

"As to that," the constable said stiffly, "I have no opinion. I should like you to come to headquarters tomorrow, early, to give me a complete statement—all you know of the case. I shall expect you to be completely frank about your own involvement."

"Happy to tell you all I know," Hewitt said in his most affable manner. "What time tomorrow?"

"As early as possible."

"Very well. Let us say seven o'clock."

An expression of alarm crossed the young constable's pink, blue-eyed, cherubic face, but he mastered it. "Oh, good, then! I shall expect you at seven. These men, I'm to take it, are your employees?"

"Yes. Art and Bill are their names. Shall you want to interview them, too?"

"Oh no. I'll want as complete a report as possible for the superintendent upon his return, but I'm sure you can give me all that."

He saluted Hewitt formally, mounted, and rode away. The Mounties were not universally liked in the Northwest Territory. The service was considered by many of the settlers and frontiersmen as a repository for the useless younger sons of wealthy, titled families—an alternative, say, for taking Holy Orders, respectable and dignified, but still just an aristocratic storehouse for surplus youth.

There was a lot of truth in that view, and young Constable Ranald Hewston was not the brightest specimen of manhood that Hewitt had ever met. But these young men went through a tough training that weeded out the weak, effete, and timid. The British Empire had been built by men who survived just such training.

Constables like Hewston walked into the most dangerous situations, contemptuously cool, and stern-voiced in giving orders to armed men with their thumbs on the hammers of their revolvers—and got away with it. "I say there, that will do, hand me that pistol!" in a soft but

overbearing voice had broken up many a potential shooting fray.

Therefore, Jefferson Hewitt did not underestimate
pink-cheeked Ranald Hewston at all, and neither, ap-
parently, did Peck. "Whew!" he said, when the Mountie
was out of sight and hearing. "Glad I don't have to spill
my guts to that one! But I see that you are able to lie with
a straight face, Mr. Hewitt."

"I told him no lies," said Hewitt. "Neither do I warn
anyone that I need only another queen to give me four of
them."

"I'll try to get your code straight in my mind as I drift
off to sleep with a full stomach for a change," said Peck.
"Personally, I have never had any objection to telling little white lies."

"Suppose we sit down together and you tell me some
big white truths," Hewitt returned. "I want to know all
you can tell me about how this occurred."

"Delighted! As I told you, I had not been easy in my
mind about the market for some time, and I sold short on
a number of stocks that I considered possible victims of a
slide. I rather—"

"Whoa! What stocks?"

"Believe it or not, Northern Pacific was one. Great
Western Land Company; Safira Silver Mines, Limited, of
Nevada; Webb-Shipley-McAllister Mining Company of
Sonora; New York, New Haven, and Hartford Railway;
McNaughten's Bank—do you want the whole list?"

"Not now. How about New York Central?"

Peck shook his finger at Hewitt. "Oh no, you don't trap
me that way! NYC may slip a little now, since the theft of

their bonds from Carlton, Brewer and Peck, but had I owned any I would have held them in a lover's clasp."

"Why did you have to go to Boston?"

"There's a dear old lady there, not much money, but what she has I made for her. You get these damned expensive obligations in my business. Every so often I had to go up and go over her investments with her. Just lonely, really."

"I see."

"You don't believe me."

"Oh, sure I believe you! As far as it goes, anyway. I just wonder why you happened to have to go to Boston *at this particular time*."

"You are a sharp one!"

Hewitt smiled mirthlessly. "Tell me about it. Good for your soul."

Peck prodded the fire thoughtfully. "Dammit," he said, "I had been suspicious of my partners for a long time, but I was juniorest and, I'm afraid, weakest in character. Afraid to have it out with them. Afraid they were up to something and I didn't know what. We had all these bonds in our own vault and various commercial vaults, and I swear, Mr. Hewitt, *I did not even know it!*"

"So, with a crisis approaching," Hewitt said, "you cut and ran for Boston and let it happen."

"Indeed not. I needed a chance to think it out and nerve myself to go to the prosecutors. It was the right move to make, believe me, only I made it too late. When I got back, the balloon had gone up."

They talked for hours. James Davidson Carlton, the senior partner, had undoubtedly been the brains of the embezzlement. He was a silent, sedate, dignified man, but, Peck had learned, he also was a crafty man. His wife had left him, taking their two teen-age daughters. His mistress had run off with another man.

"And I think she ran off with some of Jimmy's money, too," said Peck. "That was what hurt the bastard. It may have pushed him over the edge. You know, caused him to move up their schedule, do it while I happened to be out of town."

William Oscar Brewer, who now lay on a mortuary slab in Detroit, had been the youngest of the three and had put up the money to start the firm. His family had given it to him because he had failed in college, lost interest in reading law, and rejected in horror the idea of joining the Army or the Navy.

At about thirty-six he was weak of character, likable, handsome—and single. "It might surprise you," said Peck, "how many spinsters, widows, and impressionable young heiresses will buy securities recommended by a brainless pretty-boy like Oscar."

"No," said Hewitt, "I wouldn't be surprised at all. Where did you fit in, to become personal about it?"

"I was the professional. I knew the business, did the detail work, ran the office crew, visited the banks and other brokers. I did a good job. If Carlton had not been a crook and Brewer a weakling who could be bullied into Carlton's scheme, we could have been one of the most important houses in New York."

"And you had no suspicion that these bonds were in your vaults in such large quantities?"

"What do you think I am, a crook?" Peck said indignantly. "It was inconceivable to me that he could get his hands on so many of them. Our own vault was a small one; I knew we had others rented, handy to clients in certain areas—we needed them often for brief storage, sometimes just overnight. Was I expected to take a daily inventory?"

"You ran the detail work. Didn't your books show anything?"

Peck spread his hands. "Not that I remember, and when the prosecutor seized them and wouldn't let me see them—well, that's when I decided to vanish."

"Why Minneapolis? Did you have some small idea, perhaps, that Canada was where Carlton might have gone?"

"Yes, I did, because he traveled Canada for a company that printed checks for banks and also sold complete bookkeeping systems. They also printed bonds, which is how that miserable bastard got into the bond business, to my ruin and despair."

"What I'm wondering," said Hewitt, "is whether Brewer was in on it, or if he also had a hunch about Canada. Maybe he wasn't a true fugitive. Maybe he was pursuing Carlton and, unfortunately, caught up with him in Detroit."

"That thought has also occurred to me," said Peck.

~~~~~~~

Not far from where they were camped, a freelance evangelist began preaching from the back end of a rickety wagon. He had a booming voice but he was quickly drowned out by scoffers. It looked like a bigger crowd than it was, because many of them were Indians who were merely silent onlookers, probably amused by the white man's different kind of snake dance.

For there was no question about one thing—some of the whoopers in the crowd would be seeing snakes before daylight.

Peck, unruffled, mashed his new hat down over his ears and pulled his blanket up over it and went to sleep. You could not help but like the sonofagun, Jefferson Hewitt thought, but neither could you quite trust him.

He caught Bill Denny's eye and nodded at the .45 he had given him. *Don't let Peck get hold of it,* he warned with a shake of his head. Bill nodded to show that he understood.

Hewitt gave himself half an hour to ponder, while the shouting preacher competed with the hectoring drunks no more than two hundred yards away. He was looking for a man who carried a fortune in bonds and not a little cash, and who probably could commit murder coldbloodedly and cruelly. There was no question in Hewitt's mind about who had killed William Oscar Brewer.

Carlton had dumped ten thousand in cash and sixty-five thousand in bonds to get back sixty thousand, presumably in cash. Few embezzlers could retail registered bonds at more than thirty per cent of their value. Carlton already had plenty of running money and was probably on his way to Europe by now to dispose of what he had left at the customary seventy-per-cent discount.

But no one so far knew how to trace him. Maybe Ralph Elphinstone would. Hewitt had long cultivated the ability to go to sleep and wake up at exactly the hour he desired. The evangelist was still preaching when Hewitt turned on his side, and the noise was worse than ever, if possible, but he was asleep in less than two minutes.

CHAPTER SIX

He awakened promptly at six. Denny and Peck slept on. He got up, saddled and bridled his horse, and led him away without awakening them.

At the Victoria Hotel he ordered breakfast, and while it was being prepared he shaved in the public washroom and made himself as presentable as possible. He was at the North-West Mounted Police barracks five minutes before seven, where Constable Ranald Hewston and a rapid-writing clerk awaited him.

"So kind of you to come," said Hewston. "May I order tea for you? We've been awaiting you."

Hewitt had just stuffed down a big American breakfast, but you could not refuse an Englishman's tea. The orderly who brought it also brought a basket of hot muffins under a white napkin, and fresh butter. Hewitt discovered that he had some appetite left after all.

He was not entirely frank in answering Hewston's questions. The constable was obviously out of his depth in handling a big embezzlement-murder case from America, and at no time did Hewitt say, "I've got the juniorest partner of the firm with me." Had he done so, Peck would promptly have been lodged in the stout jail at the barracks and the Mountie would have taken over the case.

The constable had run out of questions without getting

a much better picture of the case, but was still doggedly seeking a path through the maze, when there came a knock at the door. He gave a visible start. Being acting commandant was a huge responsibility for the youngster, and every interruption might be another dire emergency.

This one was.

"Beg pardon, sir," the orderly said, "but there's an American here who insists on seeing Mr. Hewitt. There has been a murder, one of the chaps he was with."

Hewitt shot to his feet. The bewildered young constable looked stunned. "If you'll order your horse out, Constable," Hewitt prompted him, "I'll lead the way. It's not far."

It was Bill Denny who was waiting. He had ridden hard to get there and he was spooked by the story he had to tell. Hewitt made him wait until the Mountie appeared with his horse.

"It's Peck," said Denny. "He just kep' sleepin' after I got up. I got hungry and tried to wake him up to go to breakfast. He—he's got a big knife stuck in the back of his neck. Cut his backbone plumb in two."

"My God!" was all the young Mountie could say.

Hewitt caught Denny by the arm. "You're sure, of course, that he's dead?"

"Damn right he is. Been dead for some time, Mr. Hewitt. He's stone cold."

"The knife is still in him?"

"Yes. I left it there. I figgered the law wouldn't want anything tetched. I called over a bunch of Indians to watch the camp until I got back."

"That was the thing to do."

Hewitt swung up into the saddle. The half-dazed

young constable did likewise. Hewitt did some fast thinking as they rode.

"I didn't come entirely clean with you," he confessed as they rode. "The dead man was—or professed to be—Arthur C. Peck, of Carlton, Brewer and Peck. He's probably a fugitive, technically at least."

"Technically? Why do you say that?"

"He sold short on the market on a ten-per-cent margin, on his personal account, dealing through other brokers. Claims he cleaned up a hundred fifty thousand dollars, which he turned over to the authorities to help reduce the loss occasioned by his firm's failure. And then he skipped."

"Why?"

Hewitt shrugged. "I wish I knew. He claims he was afraid he would be convicted because of his short sales, because they would indicate previous knowledge of the embezzlement."

"I'm afraid I don't understand that. I know nothing of the securities market. If you could explain it in simpler terms, Mr. Hewitt—"

"If Carlton, Brewer and Peck went broke, and especially if it went broke through embezzlement, every stock in the market would go down in price."

"Why?"

"Because," Hewitt said impatiently, "it's a goddamned gambling game that's rigged like crooked poker. You can sell what you don't own, and Peck did that with a ten-per-cent down payment. If the price goes down, you then buy back at the lower price and pocket the profit. If you've been a fool, and the price goes up, you probably file for bankruptcy.

"Peck was afraid the authorities would think that he knew his partners were looting the firm and that he meant to come out of it with a nest egg of his own. That's the story he told me, and I'm half inclined to believe it."

"But why would he be killed? Who killed him?"

"Why, Carlton, of course, because the other partner, Brewer, has already been murdered, and Peck was the one man who could give the evidence that would enable New York to extradite Carlton from Canada to stand trial. He would have spent years in prison! You don't rook those financial sharks and get off lightly. Murder—yes, you can plead extenuating circumstances and waltz out in a few years sometimes. But the stock market? It's sacred! It demands blood sacrifices."

"I see that I have much to learn about this job," the constable said gloomily.

"You're a good learner," Hewitt said, and hoped he was right, "and you're not apt to get many cases like this one. I think you'll have a tidy package to present to your superintendent when he returns. I'm experienced at this, and if you'll let me help you, your report will have it all as straight and as complete as if the superintendent had composed it himself."

"I am in your hands."

A crowd of nearly three hundred had collected around Hewitt's camp, but a dozen or so stern, hard-faced, able-bodied Indians had surrounded it. The Indians displayed no arms, but the curious crowd displayed no interest in challenging them, either.

The crowd parted at the sight of the Mountie's resplendent uniform. Hewitt and Hewston knelt beside

Peck's body. Peck had slept half on his side and half on his face, probably with his coat collar turned up to keep his neck warm. Denny had turned him over just enough to see the knife and feel the chill in his flesh, and rigor mortis had let the body drop back into its original position the moment he had let go.

"That's just exactly the way he looked when I went over to wake him up," Denny said, his nerves and voice a little steadier now. "I guess the collar of the coat covered the knife a little better, but not much. It was darker then."

Whoever had killed Peck had approached on hands and knees, stealthily and silently, with a weapon that was not really a conventional knife. It was a piece of spring steel from a light spring wagon, one end ground down, probably on a power emery wheel, until it was no more than three quarters of an inch wide for a length of perhaps two inches. The weapon was exactly seven inches long.

The point was razor sharp, and the other end had been left as it had been on the wagon, giving it a handle about three inches long and an inch and a half wide. The killer had killed slowly, tenderly, a millimeter at a time, turning back Peck's red-checked collar to expose the bare back of his neck.

Then, gathering his strength, he had driven the crude, cruel blade in at exactly the right spot, between two vertebrae. Peck had died instantly, probably without feeling a thing, probably without any movement except a slight jerk of his body as all nerves went dead.

Getting the weapon out would have meant a tussle that

took strength. So, the murderer had merely pulled Peck's collar up to cover both the weapon and the puddle of blood.

And blood there was, for when they turned Peck over they saw that the blade had penetrated deeply enough to sever one of the carotid arteries. Cutting the spinal cord had stopped the heart; nevertheless, a considerable quantity of arterial blood had congealed under Peck's jaw.

"At least three hours ago," Hewitt said, "and probably more than that. I was awake until almost midnight. I'd get a physician to look at him, Constable, and see if he can estimate the time of death more closely."

"Yes, of course."

"There was an evangelist preaching from the tail end of a wagon yonder until after I went to sleep. He had some believers and some scoffers. Let's see if we can find anyone who was around and noticed anything."

There were plenty of witnesses. There were too many, in fact, and some of them clearly remembered things that had never happened. Naturally, Indians were the guilty ones—not just one Indian, but you had your choice of a dozen.

"Somehow," Constable Hewston said, "I can't take any of these chaps seriously. This was not done by an Indian. This was done by that man Carlton."

"Exactly right," said Hewitt. "Now, let's start looking for white men who were around the evangelist's wagon."

They talked to dozens of them, which took the entire morning. Neither believers nor scoffers had seen anything suspicious. They had noticed Hewitt's campfire, and some had been aware when it died down to darkness about midnight. The preacher had given up and driven off about half past twelve, most of them agreed.

Hewitt, Hewston, and Denny were eating lunch in the hotel restaurant when the truth suddenly hit Hewitt with the impact of a Mauser slug. He stopped eating so suddenly that he almost choked, alarming both of his companions.

"We're three damned idiots, if you'll pardon my frankness," he said. "Is there a livery stable in town?"

"Yes, of course, Barry's," said the Mountie.

"This evangelist fellow had a bony old brown team, and one of them had white front feet, I saw that much myself," said Hewitt. "I wonder if your liveryman has such a team."

"As a matter of fact," said the Mountie, "he does, but they're not often rented out. He uses them mostly for chores around the place."

"An old wagon, too? Unpainted, no end gate, no seat that I remember—anything like that?"

"Two or three, probably. He buys and sells, and by the time wagons get this far, most of them are in fairly awful condition."

"Let's go talk to him."

They lost their appetites immediately in their eagerness to interview the liveryman. They found Mr. Barry having his own lunch at home. Yes, he remembered the evangelist clearly.

"Rode one of the most beautiful black horses I've ever seen, and carried two heavy saddlebags," he said. "I put his horses up and he cautioned me to take good care of his bags. They were padlocked, by the way."

"I hope you did take good care of them," the Mountie said.

"You bet I did, but why?"

"Because," said the Mountie, "they probably contained three or four hundred thousand dollars' worth of stolen securities."

The liveryman whistled. "I thought it was funny that a preacher could ride in on a horse like that and not find a church to preach in, or some better place than a grove outside of town. But he said he was after the Indians and the drunks and roughnecks, to bring them the Light and so forth, and all he wanted was my cheapest outfit."

Hewitt felt that old thrill, the same surge of excitement that a good hunting dog must feel when he suddenly hits a hot trail. "Wonder how good a job you can do of describing him. The preacher, I mean."

"Let's see . . . I meet so damn many people! I'd say about fifty-five. Flat, dark, mean-looking face. About average size, maybe a little bigger, and I'd judge him strong as a bull elephant. Oh yes, and I think he wore false hair. You know—one of them black things, what do you call them?"

"Toupee," said Hewitt eagerly.

"That's it. Wears a forty-five that he kind of tries to keep hid under his coat, kind of like he's ashamed to preach the Gospel and go armed."

"He also carried a knife. When did he show up at your place?"

"Early yesterday morning, just as I was relieving my night man. Came back and I thought he was going to want his horse and saddlebags about four o'clock, but he told me then he was a preacher and wanted to rent my cheapest rig to preach from last night."

"Happen to know where he spent the day?"

"No, sir, I don't. I ain't in any trouble about this, am I?"

"Sir," said Hewitt, "as far as I'm concerned, you're entitled to a medal." He turned to the Mountie. "Let's see if there's a blacksmith around who remembers him."

They found the smithy quickly. Yes, just such a man had come there about mid-morning, carrying half of the broken leaf of a spring wagon. He was a woodcarver, he said, and he wanted to grind it down into a gouge.

"I found him a couple of kids to turn the emery wheel for him. He gave them a dollar apiece—can you equal that? Gave me a dollar for the use of my wheel. Best day's business them kids ever done, you can be sure of it."

They got the livery-stable night man out of his bunk above the stable. Yes, he said, the man riding the fine black horse had come in about three in the morning with the old yard team and chore wagon and had wanted his horse and saddlebags.

"I told him I didn't have no key to the safety box," the night man said, "but he said he'd pay for the padlock and hasp if I just ripped her off with a crowbar. I told him to go to hell, and the next thing I know, I'm looking down the muzzle of a forty-five.

"'Either I shoot the lock off,' the feller says, 'and shoot you too, or you rip her open.' Well, I ain't paid for that kind of a job, so I dug out the key—I knowed where it was all along—and got him his saddlebags. He paid me his bill and throwed me a dollar and rode out of here in less than twenty minutes."

"In which direction?" the Mountie said.

"I couldn't tell you, but he asked me which was the Qu'Appelle road."

"Now," Hewitt said to the Mountie, "we know which way we're going, don't we?"

〰〰〰〰〰

The North-West Mounted Police might recruit their men from spoiled darlings of the aristocracy, but they kept only the best and made policemen of them. The three of them—Hewitt, Bill Denny, and Constable Ranald Hewston—were on the trail within thirty minutes. It took Hewston just that long to change his underwear—he insisted on that—while someone saddled his horse.

Once they were on the trail, his stiffness of manner eased so considerably that even Bill began to feel comfortable with him. "I feel terribly out of my element, terribly useless, don't you know?" Hewston said. "This is an assignment that should go to a veteran, yet we're all expected to do whatever we're asked to do."

"You'll do it," said Hewitt. "What do you know of Ralph Elphinstone, the new owner of the Big C Little c?"

"Nothing. I've never met him. Never been in that area at all. Had but one assignment out of town, to apprehend a murderer in Moose Jaw, in the other direction."

"How did you make out in Moose Jaw? I hear that can be a fairly wild town, too."

"Why," said the Mountie, "there was no difficulty. Found my man, told him he was under arrest, and brought him back. I can't say he was happy. But he came."

"I understand that's what they usually do when your men put it up to them that way," said Hewitt.

Hewston frowned. "Perhaps we do rather have that reputation, but I don't regard myself as having been tested yet. Can't help but worry if I'm going to prove equal to the work. Awfully embarrassing if I failed."

"What are your duties at headquarters?"

"Usually it's local police work. Ride out and arrest chaps who have been causing trouble—knocking their wives about, shooting at neighbors, stealing cattle, things like that."

"And how do you go about arresting them?"

Ranald Hewston raised his eyebrows. "Why, that's all provided for in our manual. I first identify myself as a constable of the North-West Mounted Police, in case they can't identify me by my uniform, and then I say, 'You are under arrest and anything you say may be used against you at your trial.' If the bloke gives me trouble, I have a pair of handcuffs along. So far I've never had the chance to use them."

"Don't give up hope yet," said Hewitt.

CHAPTER SEVEN

Although Hewitt carefully deferred to the Mountie in all things, from the first it was Hewitt's command. It was his conviction that James Davidson Carlton was not hanging around Canada for the climate. He had gone to a lot of trouble to kill Art Peck. There was no question in Hewitt's mind that he would go to even more trouble to kill the two men with whom Peck had traveled—and to whom he might have talked.

That had not occurred to Hewston, but he agreed that they had to assume that Carlton would come after them and that he had money enough to recruit a renegade crew if he needed one. At times they left the main northward trail when trees or brush surrounded it, and circled the long way to keep to the open prairie. When they had to ride through ambush country Hewitt took the lead, carrying under his arm a .30-30 Henry carbine he had bought in Regina.

He led slowly, stopping to search out the trail ahead. Ranald Hewston wanted to ride rear guard, but consented to let Bill Denny take that post of next honor when Hewitt objected.

"You're too damned conspicuous in that uniform, Constable," Hewitt said. "I know that it represents real power and authority here, but we're dealing with a sly, backstabbing American who respects nothing. That red tunic would be just too tempting a target."

Three days of cautious riding brought them to the place that Sir Philip had sold to Ralph Elphinstone. Hewitt had kept a sharp eye out for the cattle branded with the Big C Little c, but he had seen few of them. The spring grass was already fetlock deep. They saw hundreds of deer and several scattered, small herds of buffalo.

But there were not enough beef cattle here to leave a mark on this range; and meanwhile, down in Texas and New Mexico and other parts of the cattlemen's West, the beef crop was rapidly outgrowing its sustenance. Here was the cowman's land of opportunity, if one existed anywhere. It was something to discuss with Conrad Meuse. It could be an investor's paradise too.

The ranch house was a big one, visible for miles. It was built of peeled poplar logs, adzed square for a weathertight fit, with a high, peaked roof of the same material, overlaid with hand-hewn cedar shakes to shed the heavy winter snows.

There was a big hay barn, and there were acres and acres of fenced corrals. Some were fenced with polewood and some were fenced with new barbwire. There were roofed shelters for the herds that did not yet exist, and from a mile away Hewitt could count over 150 fenced haystacks.

Figuring twenty tons to a stack, that was three thousand tons of hay, and probably just a fraction of what was available. Why, with enough mowing machines, bucks, and stackers, you could pile up enough hay here to winter thousands of head of cattle for spring sale. And that was when the price for prime beef was right—when everyone else was thinning out herds made lean by winter.

A big man on a spotted Indian pony came galloping to meet them. His long hair had once been red but it was almost white now. His strong face was unlined. Hewitt merely saluted him with a touch of the brim of his hat, and let Constable Hewston catch up to do the courtesies.

"Saw your red jacket," the big man said, "and told the wife I'd go out and get you if she'd get us something to eat. I suppose you're looking for McCarthy."

"As a matter of fact," said Hewston, "we are." He introduced Hewitt and Denny. The big man gave each a strong handshake. "I'm Ralph Elphinstone, and I don't mind saying I'm damned glad to see you. Maybe you can help me figure out if I've been a complete idiot or not."

Hewitt liked him immensely. He was probably seventy, but he was as vigorous and strong as a man of forty-five. Hewitt remembered Sir Philip saying that Elphinstone had married a black ex-slave who had been brought up on the Underground Railway and that he had a family. Elphinstone's accent told Hewitt two things—that he had been born in England and that he had left it early and spent most of his young manhood in the western United States.

Mrs. Elphinstone had been only fifteen when she married her white husband. She was a magnificent woman, over six feet in height, coal-black of skin and gray of hair. No fifteen-year-old slave girl could possibly have known how to read and write, let alone possess the other refinements this one had. Her voice was soft, her diction and grammar perfect. Her husband had taught her and taught her well—and she was a born learner.

The walls of the big central room were lined with books. A guitar hanging on a nail confirmed what Hewitt had deduced.

"You spent some time in Texas as a young man, didn't you?" he asked, as they waited for Mrs. Elphinstone to serve the inevitable afternoon tea.

"Yes," said Elphinstone, "but that was years and years ago. Drove a four-horse wagon team for a freight company. How the devil did you know?"

"I'm something of an expert on accents," said Hewitt. "And that's a hand-made Mexican guitar, isn't it?"

Elphinstone answered in Spanish, "Yes, it is. I have some talent with it but I never had time to learn much. I'm trying to teach my children the instrument, and they all have great talent. But, like me, they all lack time. The frontier is no place to study music."

"And yet," said Hewitt, in the same language, "there is no place where there is greater need for it. I compliment you on the paternal love which gives your children every possible advantage."

He knew that Elphinstone was probing and testing, trying to place him. He switched back to English and held out one of his business cards.

"I'm a full partner in this company," he said. "Mr. Meuse runs the office, I do the fieldwork. We have been asked to look into a big New York swindle in which we have reason to believe the man you know as McCarthy was involved."

"I've heard of your company," said Elphinstone. "I ran a bank in New Mexico for a few years."

"You must have had a remarkable career."

"Everything I know was self-taught. There are great, gaping holes in my education."

"We are the same breed of animal, then. I was practically illiterate when I joined the Army at the age of fifteen."

They were already friends. The Mountie remained silent except to thank Mrs. Elphinstone when she brought in tea and biscuits and butter. It was too formal for Bill Denny, who had fled to the stable to take care of the horses.

"These are delicious," the Mountie said, taking a second biscuit. "May I ask what they are?"

"May I answer?" said Hewitt. "They're plain baking-powder biscuits, and I'll bet Mrs. Elphinstone makes excellent light-bread, too."

"My, I haven't heard that expression in years," the black woman said. She saw the Mountie's puzzlement and explained: "I was making biscuits when I was ten years old. My mother was a kitchen woman, one of the lucky ones, because it meant we ate well. In the slave cabin they had corn bread. Risen bread baked with yeast we called 'light-bread.'"

"They still do, ma'am," said Hewitt. "May I ask if your mother escaped with you?"

The woman shook her head. "No. I never knew what became of her. I wasn't even told I was being sent to the North until three minutes before I left. They were to give out the story that I had been stolen. My mother was to wail and mourn and scar her forehead to show her sorrow. But the war was nearing its end then, and I never heard what happened."

"Cammy was getting too pretty," said Elphinstone. "The master would have taken her to town soon, to become a pleasure girl for himself and his friends."

"Cammy?" said Hewitt. "What was your last name, may I ask?"

"Slaves took the names of the families that owned them. We belonged to Mr. Preston, and my mother told me to use that name here because surely I had a right to something. Cammy—that's short for some flower that grew there, but it's so long ago I can't remember what it was."

"Camellia?"

"That's it!" she cried.

"South Carolina?"

"Yes. How did you know?"

"A trace of accent, and the camellia. They're my favorite flower, ma'am."

The woman said wistfully, "I remember that we had red ones, pink ones, white ones, mixed ones of red and pink or red and white or pink and white. I tried so long to forget so many things, and now I wish I could remember some of them. Thank you for 'Camellia,' Mr. Hewitt."

The elder son, Preston, arrived then, and soon the younger son, Colton, came in. Both were big men, like their father. Both were red-haired and copper-skinned, striking-looking, soft-voiced men of shy self-confidence. Hewitt judged them to be in their late twenties.

Before tea was over they had met the three girls. Sabine, the eldest, was one of the most beautiful women Hewitt had ever seen—tall, slim, graceful, and with an impatient intelligence that probably made life there a bore for her. She too was in her twenties. Jane was eighteen, and Leora was sixteen. All three girls were also red-haired and brown-skinned.

Mrs. Elphinstone and the young people excused themselves after tea. "The handsomest family I've ever seen, Mr. Elphinstone," said Hewitt. "Sir Philip prepared me for it, but those are amazing young people."

"My word, yes!" said Constable Hewston. "I predict a future just as handsome for them."

"Not unless the Northwest Territory is divided into self-governing provinces with representation in the Parliament at Ottawa," Elphinstone said firmly. "Yes, Constable, I'm one of the 'radicals' who are demanding either provincial status or secession for the prairie nations."

A certain coldness came over the constable's face. "I am not permitted to discuss politics, sir," he said. "All I do is enforce the law."

"Yes," said Elphinstone, "but I imagine you'll make a complete report when you return to Regina, and you may want to say that the Elphinstones and all their neighbors within one hundred miles unanimously—unanimously, sir! —demand provincial status."

The Mountie nodded stiffly. "Secession" was a bad word east of the great Canadian prairie, because back there the politicians knew that if the so-called Prairie Provinces declared themselves to be either one free nation or many, union with the United States would soon follow. No one had forgotten the example of Texas.

It could become a strain that might hamper the development of working relations with the owner of the Big C Little c. And suddenly a serious strain might develop at any moment, Hewitt saw when Bill Denny at last was persuaded to come in for supper.

That gorgeous girl, Sabine, stared at Bill as though beholding a god. She could not take her eyes off him, and Bill, who had not looked at another woman since his wife's death, stared at her like a man awakening to life from an endless bad dream.

"Now, to business," said Elphinstone, after supper. "There's lots of talk about. A man on his way down from Prince Albert last week told me he heard that McCarthy sold me this property for fifteen thousand dollars less than he paid for it three weeks earlier."

Hewston let Hewitt carry the burden of talk. "And that naturally puzzled you."

"Not much, really. Sir Philip is a headstrong old codger. Takes advice from no one. Trusts his own judgment and instinct to the disaster point. A born sucker, if Constable Hewston will excuse my use of that word in connection with a baronet."

"I'm afraid you're right, sir," said Hewston.

"I'm sure something was crooked," said Elphinstone, "but I haven't figured out what. I'm hoping you are about to enlighten me."

"We'll try," said Hewitt. "First, how secure is your title? Other things being equal, I don't see how you can lose property you bought and paid for in good faith."

"My solicitor in Regina tells me that I have no worry; that if there is a loss, Sir Philip must take it—as he damn well should," said Elphinstone. "However, just in case of something shady, I protected myself by paying thirty thousand dollars by draft on the Volney bank, and gave a ninety-day note for the other thirty thousand. It's not due for a couple of months, but I expect to see him sooner."

Hewitt felt the stirrings of one of those hunches. "Why?"

"After the deal was made," Elphinstone said, carefully and slowly, "and I thought we had seen the last of Mr.

McCarthy until the note was due, he came back. In my absence! In the absence of my two sons! He knew we were heading east immediately to try to buy cattle."

He paused, eyes narrowing, color ebbing from his pink, healthy-looking face.

"However," he went on, "Preston was convinced that McCarthy was infatuated with my eldest daughter, Sabine. Perhaps he saw things that I did not see, or sensed things that I did not sense.

"After some argument with me, Preston abandoned the trip with Colton and me and came home. He was right. The—the circumstances were outrageous. He'll kill McCarthy if he ever gets a second chance. . . ."

wwwww

The red-haired, brown-skinned man had reached home late in the afternoon. He approached his own house stealthily—and, sure enough, there were the tracks of a strange, shod horse. They came from the south, and there was no return trail.

Preston Elphinstone circled the house and came in from behind the haystacks and barns, dismounted, and led his horse. He saw a big black stallion securely tied with both bridle reins and halter rope at the corner of the big hay barn. Behind the saddle was the usual bedroll that the cowboys called a soogan. There was also a big, flat, black case of thick, soft leather. He could see the glint of brass hasps and padlocks on it.

The stallion saw or smelled Preston's horse and blared a challenge. Preston quickly led his horse behind the barn and tied it. He got his holster and .45 out of his own soogan and walked around the barn to a calf pen where there was a small door into the barn.

He went in and walked down the aisle between the high stacks of pressed and matted hay. He heard his sister's voice before he saw anything.

"You contemptible sonofabitch!" She was panting. "Lay hands on me and my father and brothers will have your bones bared with a whip."

"Please, Sabine, listen to me," came McCarthy's quivering voice. "I mean you no harm. I love you! And I'm rich enough to dress you in the best and put you in your proper position in life."

"Stand back, or by God I'll whip you myself!"

Preston heard a scuffle, a grunt of pain from McCarthy, and then a shriek of anger and outrage from Sabine. He began running. He rounded the end of the hay and there they were on the ground.

Sabine still had the Indian-made, braided deerskin quirt in her hands, but Preston saw McCarthy jerk it away from her with his right hand. With his left he caught the collar of the girl's dress and hauled her to her feet.

Preston fired just as McCarthy swung the quirt. He was not a gunman and he came as close to hitting his sister as he did her assailant.

McCarthy dropped the quirt and went for the .45 in his coat pocket. He and Preston fired at the same time, but neither was hit. Then Sabine stooped, snatched up the quirt, and brought it down savagely across McCarthy's back.

He shrieked and ran, and Preston chased after him,

thumbing back the hammer of his .45. He was trembling with a murderous rage, and even when he clutched the .45 in both hands to steady it, he missed.

But he came close enough to drive McCarthy away on foot, with no chance to untie and mount his powerful black stallion. Preston pursued him toward the northwest, reloading and firing whenever he thought he saw movement in the brush. At last he lost him.

~~~~~~

"Colton and I heard the shooting and came back," Elphinstone said. "He had torn Sabine's clothing a little but he hadn't hurt her. We locked his stud horse up in our one box stall, hid his saddle and bridle, and brought his bedroll and suitcase into the house.

"But we underestimated him. We had a watchdog I thought would let us know if anything moved outside. Somehow this fellow lay for him and brained him with a club. He pried the lock off the box stall and got his horse. He stole one of our bridles and one of our saddles.

"But I've an idea he'll be back for whatever is in that case. Anything that's brass-bound and locked with two padlocks—well, that's not a quart of snakebite remedy."

"I think Constable Hewston should take charge of that immediately," Hewitt said. "I believe it is your legal responsibility to turn the case over to him and for him to open it in the presence of witnesses."

"I'll be glad to be rid of the thing," said Elphinstone, "but I don't much look forward to having McCarthy prowling my place again at night."

"Well," said Hewitt, "he's on his way, I think on the same fine horse, with a new saddle and a new set of saddlebags. I move that we nominate ourselves as a committee of welcome, with one able-bodied, armed man on duty outside the house every hour of the day and night. Now, let's see that case."

Preston brought it into the room. It was beautifully made of finely tanned pigskin, well dyed, and had the finest brass mountings. The padlocks were small ones but good ones. McCarthy—or Carlton—had bought the best, and it was a cinch they would both open with the same key.

It took Hewitt almost thirty minutes to pick them with the tools available there—part of a springy corset stave filed down, a couple of bent hairpins, and an awl with a long tine made of particularly hard steel.

Inside the case were five bundles of neatly sorted papers—heavy, rag-bond paper printed in ornate green, purple, and crimson inks. They counted them twice, carefully—$265,000 in railroad, steamship, corporation, canal, and public-improvement bonds.

CHAPTER EIGHT

Some critical decisions had to be made—now.

There were only fourteen bondholders' names. The largest single possessory interest was fifty thousand dollars—the smallest, forty-five hundred. Of the fourteen bondholders, nine were women. Now Hewitt wished he were close enough to the telegraph wires to have Conrad Meuse's help. As it was, his best guess was that somebody in the firm—possibly Brewer, certainly Carlton, maybe even Peck—had persuaded every widow and spinster they knew to plunge their life savings into these bonds.

The big one—fifty thousand dollars—was a trusteeship, "Asa P. MacManus, trustee for Eulalia Murphy, a minor." Some old man, no doubt, made responsible for the estate of a child, and looking for expert advice when he came to the firm of Carlton, Brewer and Peck.

The bonds had all been transferred within the last fifty days. The nominal owners would not yet have reason to worry, because a trustworthy firm had not yet turned over the actual bonds bought for their accounts. Sometimes it took three months—sometimes six months.

At least $100,000 had vanished, and probably more. The bearer bonds had gone first, naturally. Sir Philip Quarles was stuck for $40,000 in bonds with false endorsements—Franklyn Patterson of Volney Private Bank, Ltd., another $40,000. Hewitt estimated that Carlton, alias Vincent McCarthy, had at least $100,000 in cash.

Two things had to be done. Carlton had to be caught, and that money, whatever the sum, had to be recovered. And the $265,000 in bonds had to be brought safely back and returned to the rightful owners in New York.

"This chap has played a lone hand so far," Constable Ranald Hewston said thoughtfully. "He hasn't done badly, but surely it's apparent to him by now that this is no longer a one-man job."

"My feelings exactly," said Hewitt. His respect for the Mountie grew greater, the better he got to know him. There were a lot of things he didn't know, but he wanted to learn and he had as cool a head as any man Hewitt had ever known.

Hewston looked at Ralph Elphinstone. "Neighbors are few and far between here, aren't they?" he asked.

"Yes," said the rancher, "but we have friends who will help."

"How far away?" Hewitt asked. "And what about people you don't trust, who might be hired to help rob you? As I see it, we've got to muster men enough to do three things."

Darkness had fallen and Preston, Colton, and Bill Denny had done the milking and the other evening chores. Mrs. Elphinstone now called them to supper. They continued the conversation over two roasted wild turkeys and the last of last year's potato crop.

From now on, until they got a garden in and it began yielding, the Elphinstones would live on wild game and the milk and eggs from their own cows and chickens. But that was the way big fortunes were built in a country as new and rich and productive as this one.

"You were saying we had three things to do," Elphin-stone said.

"Actually, four," said Hewitt. "We've got to maintain sentry-go over this place continuously until we pick this scamp up and put him in irons."

Elphinstone smiled. "You'll notice that Preston isn't eating with us," he said. "Colton will relieve him later. I imagine it would be rather tricky for this chap to slip up on either of my boys at night."

"And I'll relieve Colton later," said Hewitt. "No, let's not argue. I have good night vision and do some of my best thinking in the dark. And then Constable Hewston will relieve me before daylight. Right now, the important thing is to keep this house and these women safe."

"And the next thing?"

"With all respect to Constable Hewston," said Hewitt, "my opinion is that we've got to keep these stolen bonds here, guarded along with the house, until we can safely send them to Regina with enough men to be sure they get there. So let's think of the bonds as third place."

"What's second place?" asked Elphinstone.

"Catch or kill—and I much prefer catching—this murdering thief of a Carlton, or McCarthy as you knew him."

"First?"

"Get the men who can do it, somehow."

The Elphinstone family sat down and made a list of all the settlers they knew who lived within a day's ride. They came up with the names of eighteen able-bodied men. The trouble was, many of them had wives, children, houses, and livestock of their own to protect.

"This ought to be a single-man's country," Hewitt said. "Let's go through and pencil out all the names of the men with responsibilities."

That left them with ten names. Two of these men had
wives, but they had only shanties to live in and their
wives could be brought to the Elphinstone place until
their safety at home could be guaranteed again.

They made two lists of good men. Hewitt would take
one and travel with Colton Elphinstone and Bill Denny.
Constable Hewston would take the other and would be
accompanied by the eldest son, Preston.

"Between Cammy, Sabine, and myself," Elphinstone
said, "I guarantee we'll be safe here. Jane's pretty good
with a Winchester Seventy, too. She got her deer last
fall."

Hewitt and Hewston slept in one of the back bedrooms
of the big log house. The nights had turned warm, and
the first generation of mosquitoes had already become
adults, so they slept under netting canopies.

At two-thirty in the morning, Hewitt arose and, carrying his boots, tiptoed through the house. He met Colton
just coming to awaken him, Colton carrying the Winchester his father had mentioned. Hewitt refused it. He
preferred his own Henry .30-30 for this work. It was
lighter, faster to operate, and its killing range was greater
than a man's eyesight in the dark.

The big, rough-haired brown dog that usually slept
with the livestock fell in step behind him as he prowled
the house, around and around, keeping in cover as well as
he could. Sir Philip had planned for his house to set in a
big park of grass with only one decorative clump of trees
near it, but had sold it before clearing all the brush.

There were plenty of hiding places where a man could
crouch and fire from ambush, but a shot would stir out
every sleeping man in the house. A knife or a garrote was

more likely, but the presence of the dog reduced the danger of that.

By now Hewitt had a pretty good mental picture of the man he was dealing with. He was a schemer but not a brilliant one; any fool could high-pressure old ladies and senile trustees into buying enough blue-chip bonds to accumulate a mass of them.

He was coldblooded. Not only did he deliberately rob old women, he garroted one of his partners and stabbed the other with a ghastly, lethal weapon he had made with his own hands from a piece of spring steel found in a frontier junkpile.

He could plan ahead, but in a rut. He could not get away from names starting with *C* when he changed from one to another. Hewitt remembered that first discussion with Peck about going to Canada, about the Big C Little c Ranch. He had called it the Casewell place.

Perhaps Peck had been in on the thefts, after he had seen that Carlton had already ruined the firm and that there was no future for him in New York. Probably there had been correspondence between Sir Philip and Carlton, or at least Carlton had heard that the magnificent property was for sale.

"See you at the Casewell ranch, because that's the name I'll be using after I buy it, and we'll split up," Carlton had said. Something like that. And then he had either forgotten about "Casewell" to become "Vincent McCarthy," or, what was more likely, he had never intended to let Peck catch him there.

Buy at the seller's price and sell at the buyer's—any way to make a fast deal. No matter what loss he took, it was with stolen money. And in any case, if his scheme went through he would still get more out of the bonds than if he had fenced them on the London or Paris market.

Or had Peck really been in pursuit of the man who had betrayed him and given him the name of thief? Had Peck been on the level all along? Had he picked up the Casewell name in some of the papers in the office before he skipped New York?

It bothered Hewitt not a little. Recognizing all of Peck's shams and weaknesses, Hewitt still felt a lingering, hangdog liking for the fellow, and his death had been a sad ending to a pretty fair life a misfit had built for himself. *If,* that is, his story could be believed.

At daylight, Preston and Jane Elphinstone came out to milk the cows and feed the horses, chickens, and hogs. Hewitt curried and brushed his horse, saddled him, and, carrying the .30-30 under his arm, rode around the place in an ever-widening circle.

He did not claim to be a tracker—not like some of the old codgers he had hired to track for him—but he was sure that Carlton, alias McCarthy, probably alias Casewell too—had not been near the place. He saw some good cattle, shorthorns mostly, with Elphinstone's brand, the little *c* within the big one.

By the time he got back to the house, breakfast was ready and their trail lunches were packed. They were eager to get going on their search for able-bodied men to help them catch Carlton.

"Something seems to be on your mind, Mr. Hewitt," Elphinstone said, as they ate.

"Yes," said Hewitt, "there is. I wonder if you ever heard

of a certain Jim Casewell. Sorry, but that's all the name I have for him."

"There's a James J. Casewell in Ottawa, a landbroker," said Elphinstone. "In fact, McCarthy bought this place through him and I used him to buy it from McCarthy."

"How did you and Sir Philip get in touch with him?"

"I was farming south of Winnipeg, and I saw his notices in the newspapers. All my life I've saved my money for just such a place as this, and he described several that sounded suitable. I wrote to him."

"And?"

"He wrote back that he had just sold this place for Sir Philip but that the buyer was unhappy and would probably take a loss. Suggested I come see him and make my own deal. No fee. I thought that was damned decent of him."

A strange look crossed his face. He got up and went into the big front room, which was the living room as well as his office, and came back with a pack of letters tied with string.

"I saved all my correspondence," he said. "If you suspect what I think you suspect—"

No question about it, the Casewell handwriting and the McCarthy handwriting were identical. They were even in the same black ink. The first Casewell letter was dated more than a year ago.

"No spur-of-the-moment, grab-and-snatch theft, anyway," Hewitt said.

"The one consolation," said Elphinstone, a little ruefully, "is that Sir Philip was taken in worse than I. He paid the man a thousand pounds for commission. When I bought from McCarthy, he mumbled around about how I ought to pay half the commission, but you can bet I shut him up on that in a hurry."

Within an hour the men were on their way. Hewitt, Bill Denny, and Colton headed north, toward the Qu'Appelle. He had heard that its valley was one of the most beautiful places in the world, and it was. The silvery river was past the spring-flooding stage, and traced a glittering, serpentine path down the rich, flat valley. From the heights above, where Colton Elphinstone, Hewitt and Denny sat their horses, it looked too beautiful to be real.

They returned three days later, leading an armed entourage of five men and two women. The women would be guests of the Elphinstones until it was over. One, a Mrs. Flaherty, was a diminutive, gray-haired woman who carried a Winchester of her own.

"We'd no sooner got our house built," she said, "than me old man run off wid another woman. So be damn to him, says I—I'll run me own farm."

It was she who brought down the deer with a spine shot from horseback when they were within ten miles of Elphinstone's place. She would, Hewitt decided, add considerably to the defense forces left at home.

Constable Hewston and Preston Elphinstone had already arrived, with an ominous report. They had brought back three able-bodied fighting men and one young woman, newly widowed. Hewitt did not see her, since Mrs. Elphinstone had taken her into the bedroom.

Hewston told them what had happened.

"This bounder, Carlton," he said, "has already recruited a gang of at least four. They came to this poor woman's house the other day and demanded food. She had but a little tea in the house, and bread in the oven. Her husband was out hunting meat then.

"They became enraged and began to abuse her. It didn't get as far as rape, because her husband came home in time. He shot one of them through the arm before two of them got him in the head and chest. The poor woman saw him murdered before her eyes."

"What then?" Hewitt asked.

"The leader—undoubtedly Carlton—still wanted to have his way with her. But the others were frightened off. Hadn't planned on murder, they said. She must have been out of her head for almost a day before we got there, buried her husband, and persuaded her to come along with us."

"If we hadn't known what we were up against," Hewitt said, "we do now. Constable, there are you and Bill and I, and Preston and Colton, and these eight fine neighbors. I'd say you have a hell of a force and that this bastard hasn't much happiness to look forward to."

The Mountie's face betrayed his uneasiness. "I've no experience in command, Mr. Hewitt," he said. "I'd prefer that you lead us and give the orders."

Hewitt shook his head. "Not in Canada. Nobody ranks the North-West Mounted Police. But if I can serve you as adjutant, Constable, it will be my pleasure."

Hewitt's hazel eyes met Hewston's clear blue ones, and the color came back to the Mountie's cheeks. "Very well," he said, "I'll accept your kind offer. Any order you give will be in my name, and I'll take the responsibility for it."

CHAPTER NINE

That evening, about an hour after dark, the big dog set up a fierce baying. Elphinstone quickly blew out the lamp while Preston reached for a shotgun. Then they heard the angry barking of another dog, farther away, and the faint halloo of a man.

"Sounds like Louie," Elphinstone said in a voice that betrayed both hope and relief. "By God, wouldn't that be a bit of luck! Mr. Hewitt, you and Preston slip outside with me. Let's not be tricked."

They went out the side door. Elphinstone listened to the other dog for a moment and then chuckled. "Come on in, Louie," he shouted. "I'll hold this fellow so there won't be a dogfight."

He got a good grip on the dog's collar. A man leading a big dog on a chain came rapidly toward them. He stood well over six feet, yet Hewitt doubted that he carried more than 145 pounds. In the dark he appeared bearded, ragged, and unkempt. He was hatless and wore moccasins.

"I heared ye was havin' trouble, Ralph," he said, "and I made the sign of six fellers that sure wa'n't lookin' for homesteads over on Bradbury Creek. Reckoned I'd throw in with ye if I's welcome."

"You are indeed," Elphinstone said, wringing the man's

hand again. "I'd rather have you than a regiment of cavalry. Come inside and meet everybody, Louie."

"Louie," said Preston, "I'm so glad to see you I could cry!"

"Oh, shoot! You'll be a lot gladder to see my back when I leave, Pres."

They went inside. Louis Fuller was a throwback, perhaps the last of his kind. His father had come from New England to trap in the northern country, and in his old age he had married a Cree girl. Hewitt calculated rapidly in his mind: Louie seemed to be in his forties. His father must have been about sixty when Louie was conceived.

A hundred years ago, then, Louie Fuller's father had been a lone wilderness man, no doubt a Loyalist fugitive from the American Revolution who could not settle down among the urban citizens of Canada.

"So you're policemen, air ye?" he said when he was introduced to Hewitt and Constable Hewston. "Well, I'm on t'other side. I'm a thief."

"That so?" Hewitt said, liking him instantly. "What do you steal?"

"Whatever I need," Louie said cheerfully. "Right now I'm lookin' to steal a horse and some clothes. Where I come from, I git by on foot and nobody keers how I look. But if I'm goin' to associate myself with the law, I better git into costume, hey?"

"We've got clothes that will fit you," said Preston. "Even moccasins."

The Mountie did not know what to make of him. The big dog, which appeared to be half mastiff and half hound of some kind, kept close to his master for a mo-

Wrangell Public Library
Dead Eye 91

ment. Hewitt stood with his palm out and in a moment the dog came over and sniffed it. Then he began sniffing all around him and finally sat down beside him.

"There ye air!" said Louie. "Ye've made a friend of him, and he's choosy about his friends. Now, if your missus would just bait me up, Ralph, and find some scraps for old Benedict thar—"

They laid plans as they ate. It was Hewitt's suggestion that Constable Hewston and two reliable men start back to Regina on fast, tough horses with the black bag of bonds. "Put them in Mr. Patterson's bank vault," Hewitt advised, "and wire your superintendent the story so far. We'll form a posse comitatus and try to bring in this wretch and his recruits."

"I rather feel that my duty is here," the young Mountie said dubiously.

"If I may say so," Elphinstone put in, "you represent official authority, and your duty is to get back to headquarters and get the full weight of the majesty of British law into this matter. We're not dealing with an isolated chicken thief or trapline robber, Constable. Here is an extremely dangerous murderer who, it seems, has raised a gang of five. That's a small army in these parts, and the peace has already been violently broken. I think it's your duty, Constable, to apprise Ottawa of the full facts."

The Mountie agreed reluctantly. He wanted to be in on the pursuit and capture, but this time his scarlet tunic marked him for what was practically staff work. He hated it, but one thing he had been taught was that duty was duty.

They slept all over the floor that night, Hewitt on a

bearskin in the corner of the big living room. He woke long before daybreak, hearing low voices nearby. He did not mean to eavesdrop but he could not help it.

It was Constable Ranald Hewston and Ralph Elphinstone's red-haired, brown-skinned daughter, sitting by the fireplace, and as far as Hewitt could tell, the girl's right hand was in both of the Mountie's.

"No," Hewston was saying in his cultivated English voice, "I have never thought myself in love. It is a new sensation to me, Miss Sabine."

"You'll be many, many times in love before you meet the woman you'll marry," came Sabine's soft reply.

"Not I," said Hewston. "I—I know my many shortcomings. I am a poor worm socially, always the odd man in any company. I spend most of my time with my own thoughts, and I believe I have learned to know myself as few men do. And believe me, Miss Sabine, I am desperately and devotedly in love with you. Can't you believe that?"

"I don't know what to say, Constable," the girl said in a troubled voice. "We come from two different worlds, and while you may—"

"Please!" he interrupted. "You mustn't think in those terms. You are you and I am I, and that's all that counts. All I want is your permission to ask your father if I may call on you while you make up your mind."

"It would mean the end of your career."

"And the start of a new one. I feel at home here as I never felt at home with my own family. I've a little money, so I would not be a parasite. The service is full of outcasts of various kinds. Outcasts who have no family ties that mean anything make the best mounted policemen. I love the service but I love you even more, and I want to speak to your father."

The girl stood up. Hewston rose with her, still holding her hand.

"Do as you like about speaking to Dad, but I think he'll only remind you of the differences that will keep us apart," she said sadly.

"Oh, Miss Sabine!"

"Constable, please—!"

"Ranald, call me Ranald."

"It—it's crazy, Ranald. My mother's a black woman. We're slave stock. Your family—"

The young man lost his head and threw his arms around her, and as far as Hewitt could tell, the gorgeous girl did not put up much of a fight. They kissed long and lingeringly, until, breathless, she tore herself away.

"No, you've got to be on the trail early in the morning and so have I," she said. "No more of this, Ranald. You must think—*think*, man! And so must I."

"I have already thought. I *know*," said Hewston.

The girl ran from the room. The Mountie sat down on the big stone hearth and lit a cigar. By the light from his match, Hewitt saw that he had taken off his scarlet tunic and wore his suspenders over his undershirt—"vest," the English called it. He needed a shave. Something had aged him so that he looked forty-five instead of twenty-two or -three or whatever he was.

Crisis did that to people. Some people, crisis destroyed —others found their true selves. Hewitt had a hunch that this young fellow, though he might not be the brightest in the world, was a good deal of a man. Too good a man, he decided, to be spied on.

He sat up on the bearskin. "Constable," he said.

Hewston leaped to his feet. "Mr. Hewitt?" he replied, peering about blindly in the dark. "You were listening. That was—beastly!"

Hewitt rose, and in his socks crossed the big room toward the fireplace. "It would be, my boy," he said, "if it had been intentional. *You* invaded *my* privacy, and what I overheard was not of my design."

Hewston stood rigid with embarrassment and anger. "I deserve your contempt, Mr. Hewitt," he said, "but I hope you will remember the young lady's good repute, and that she deserves better than to be made the subject of gossip."

"I'll go even further than that, Hewston," Hewitt said. "She deserves to be swept off her feet—carried away against her will—courted impetuously and forcefully— wooed wildly and fiercely, and not like a nice English boy woos a girl. If you don't do it, whatever her father thinks, you're going to lose out on the finest wife a man could have."

"My God, Hewitt, do you really feel that?" the Mountie cried.

"Yes," said Hewitt, "and, having been dragged into it, I'll add that you'd better get cracking before she catches her breath. Trap her, corner her—it won't be as hard as you think!—and smother her with kisses before you leave for Regina in the morning."

The constable wiped the sweat from his face with his bare forearm. "Mr. Hewitt," he said in a voice that shook, "I have always been schooled to control my emotions, but my feelings for Miss Sabine and my extreme gratitude to you—" He choked up.

Hewitt said, "What you need is a stiff drink to steady

your nerves and make you realize it's not all a dream. I saw where Ralph hid the whiskey bottle. Ever drink from the neck of a bottle?"

"Why—why, I think so."

Hewitt led the way through the darkness to the little cabinet in the corner where he had seen Elphinstone put a half-gallon bottle of scotch malt whiskey. He felt for it in the dark, found it, and removed the cork.

"It is my privilege to drink to you first," he said, tipping back the bottle. "To your happiness with Miss Sabine, sir —to your continued good fortune—to your future, which I deem very happy indeed, as the founding father of a clan of splendid citizens in this wonderful new land."

He took his drink and handed the bottle to the Mountie. Plainly, Hewston was too overcome to know what to say. "To your very good health," he finally got out, "with my most affectionate gratitude, sir."

They had eaten before daylight, and Elphinstone had picked two good men to accompany Hewston to Regina with the bonds. They were given the three fastest, toughest horses bearing the Big C Little c brand, a day's rations, a Winchester rifle, and three .45 revolvers with plenty of ammunition.

"My land, where *is* that girl?" Mrs. Elphinstone said as she was serving breakfast. "She has never failed me before."

"She's going to Regina, and so am I, Cammy," Mr. Elphinstone said. "You'll be perfectly safe here and we'll need all the help we can get on the trail. There's no better woodsman—no, and no better horseback shot!—in Canada than Sabine."

"Yes," said her mother, "but where has she vanished, just when she's needed?"

Hewston was missing too, and Hewitt had his own ideas. Somewhere in this big, rambling house, the aristocratic Mountie had followed his advice. He had hurled aside his gentlemanly British reserve and no doubt was silencing Sabine's protests with the only successful technique.

No woman, Hewitt had long ago discovered, could keep on arguing while she was being kissed, especially if she wanted to be kissed.

Louie Fuller was eager to be on the trail. The sun was not yet up when the saddled horses were led to the door. Sabine appeared, wearing men's clothing and a worried, troubled, guilty look. She was munching a sandwich. A moment later the Mountie came out, in full uniform, carrying the black case under his arm. Hewitt had padlocked it again so that it might appear never to have been lock-picked and opened. His two escorts were waiting impatiently.

Elphinstone helped him tie the case containing the $265,000 in bonds on behind his saddle. "Mount up and be on your way, Constable," he said, "and the best of luck to you. Don't kill those horses, but use them hard. They can go and go and go."

"Sir," said Hewston, "if I could have three minutes of your time alone—"

"I'll talk to him," Hewitt interposed. "Be on your way with the boodle."

Unless the bonds were recovered, the fee of BB&I

might be small indeed. A man had to keep his eye on business even during someone's agonizing *crise de coeur,* or one might even say especially then.

⁕⁕⁕⁕⁕⁕

They had, Hewitt thought, sufficient forces. Of the eight men he and Colton and Denny and Preston and Hewston had recruited, two were too old to stand the hard life of what might be a long trail. They were left behind to guard the property, with the help of Mrs. Flaherty, who might prove to be the equal of any of them.

That left six, plus Louie Fuller. Two of them went with Constable Hewston on the fast ride to Regina with the bonds. That left Hewitt, in nominal command, the three Elphinstones, Louie Fuller, and four of the neighbors recruited for the chase.

And then there was Bill Denny, who was so easily overlooked because of his quiet ways, shyness, and habit of going where the work was. He looked more boyish than ever this morning, yet Hewitt thought he could be as tough as he had to be.

Looking them over as they rode out, Hewitt thought he had never had such good men under his orders before. It was at least an hour's ride, Louie said, to where he had picked up the sign of the Carlton gang. Hewitt used that time to get Elphinstone aside and tell him, quite frankly, what he had seen, heard, and advised.

"I'll lose them all eventually," Elphinstone said, "but I never thought I'd lose one to a nephew of Lord Byrd, especially the one who is his lordship's pet."

"Who is Lord Byrd?"

"Rich, headstrong, influential, and sometimes a damned scoundrel," said Elphinstone. "Ranald's his youngest. Inherited quite a bit of money from his mother's people. Damm it, doesn't the boy realize how my girl will be treated by those dummies?"

"I believe he has plans to move in with you," said Hewitt. "I think he wants to invest in your ranch and become a partner and cut his ties back home."

"Oh, he does, does he? I'm to get not just a damned aristocratic son-in-law, but one with money to look down his nose at me. Mr. Hewitt, how does the fellow strike you, anyway?"

"He has lots to learn," said Hewitt, "but he's a learner. The main thing is, even if nothing comes of it, your daughter has the right to be courted. To be able to look back and remember her first romance. However it works out, it will be for the best."

"Well," Elphinstone sighed, "Cammy will have the last word on it. She can see through a man and she has influence that I don't have with the girl."

"My money is on Sabine to make up her own mind," said Hewitt.

"I'm afraid you're right." Elphinstone sighed again, this time a sigh of hopeless resignation. "A man with marriageable daughters on a frontier has a problem, Mr. Hewitt. And I already have enough problems."

CHAPTER TEN

"Don't call him Benny," said Louie Fuller. "His name is Benedict Arnold. His sire's name was Benedict Arnold. His sire's sire was named Benedict Arnold. I'll help recover your damned Yank bonds and catch your Yank crooks, but if ye make light of my dog's name, I'll get an anger on me."

"You know what you are, Louie?" Hewitt asked.

Fuller's swarthy face grew darker yet. "What?"

"You like to pretend you're a man of spirit and conviction, but to me you're just a man who likes trouble, and the more of it the better."

Fuller looked at him a minute and then laughed. "Maybe ye be right," he said. "God knows, everything's so tame there's naught but duty and work left in the world."

He pointed ahead to where a thick growth of alders and lighter brush, probably sumac, marked a creek. "There's where they camped. They shot a deer. Benedict was on its trail when suddenly we came to where they'd butchered it. I put him back on his chain and we took it sly from there on. But they had already et their grub and moved on. And, says I to meself, it's time now to go see Ralph Elphinstone."

Just in case Carlton and his gang were still lurking along the creek, Hewitt had his men spread out and approach slowly, riflemen at each end, covering a line nearly a mile long. The big, ugly dog ran free, but Louie could bring him back with a single piercing whistle. Benedict went straight to the cold camp sign he had found yesterday.

It was still cold. The wolves had taken the bones of the deer. Not a spark was left in the ashes. Louie showed them the tracks he had seen yesterday and how he had counted six separate horses.

Only one horse was shod all around. That would be Carlton's big black. The others rode cow-ponies or horses stolen from Indians or farmers. It did not take much money to buy men like these riders.

It was too cold for Benedict to follow the scent, but Louie seemed to see the track anyway. The gang had headed south, Louie said. They had rested their horses and now would be pushing them hard.

"Trying to get between us and Regina," he said. "I'd wager that puts it up to the gentleman in the purty pink coat before the day is over. They'll butt heads with them afore we kin."

"I'm afraid so," Hewitt agreed. He wished now that he had insisted that a larger party be in charge of getting the loot back to the safety of the Volney bank.

But they could not chance shortcuts. They had to stay with the trail that Louie had found for them—found as much by instinct as anything else. They did not often see the tracks of the six outlaws, but just when they were ready to decide they had guessed wrong, Louie would find where they had crossed a slough still muddy from the spring runoff, or where they had stopped to rest their horses and let them tear at the sweet, new grass.

They took a chance that their horses were far better,

and pushed a little harder, with less rest. They ate in the saddle—Louie in the lead, Hewitt beside and a little behind him so that they could consult together, and Elphinstone commanding the group behind. His daughter was merely one of the members of the posse. She wore a man's checked shirt and Levi's and boots. A .45 was too big for her hand, but there was a Winchester model 70 lashed to her saddle. It was not an ornament.

Constable Ranald Hewston was not the only man intoxicated by the red-haired, brown-skinned girl. Hewitt himself was aware of her every second of every minute and every minute of every hour. Sabine was not just beautiful. There were women with prettier faces and more inflammatory bodies, but this girl was still, pure beauty, like the streaking of a comet across the sky.

Louie Fuller was capable of intense concentration. He and Benedict, the dog, which he now allowed to run free, were like two parts of a single organism. Louie could twist his lips and emit a short, piercing whistle almost like the sound of a bird, and Benedict would hear it and it would mean something to him and he would obey. It was always the same signal, but somehow the dog knew if it meant *Slow down,* or *More to the right,* or *Take a look along the creek there.*

The single gunshot came from so far away that Hewitt was not sure he'd heard it until he saw Louie haul in his horse and look around.

"Where y' think it come from?" he snapped.

Hewitt pointed straight south. "There."

One by one Louie polled the others. Some had not heard it at all, and the others were sure it had come from the south.

"Let's go!" said Louie. "We let the sonofabitch outfox

us. He laid for the constable on a beeline, and we've been following decoy tracks laid by his gang."

They dug in their spurs. They heard another shot, and then another, but they were from a different gun. Somebody was firing back. A few moments later, they heard the crack of the first gun again and a quick reply from the second.

A fleet little cow-pony with "hot blood" of some purebred strain in her forged up beside Hewitt's horse. It was Sabine, and in her heart she was probably in terror, but her fury was greater than her fear. Louie looked back and shouted at her:

"No! You'll just knock your horse out, girl. Stay behind Mr. Hewitt."

"You go to hell!" she shouted back.

Louie and Hewitt dug in their spurs and, on their bigger horses, simply ran off from her. Hewitt looked back to Elphinstone to motion *Spread out, form a front!* Men began peeling off right and left, covering an ever-widening area.

A rider appeared fleetingly as he crossed a brushy, wet-weather creek a mile away. "Oh my God," Sabine wailed as he vanished.

She yanked the straps that held the Winchester and slid a cartridge into the chamber. She dropped the reins on her mare's neck and guided her with her knees, lashing her with the quirt. The game little horse spurted forward.

"Stay with her!" Louie shouted at Hewitt. Hewitt nodded, and when Sabine swung sharply to the left in an effort to intercept the rider, he went with her. He pulled up briefly beside the girl to call to her over the drumming of their horses' feet.

"Don't kill your horse, miss," he said. "We'll get him, never fear. Take it easy."

"I want a shot at him," she said, almost sobbing. "Just one, from within range, and I don't care if I kill a dozen horses to do it."

"You haven't got a dozen to kill, my dear. You have just this one."

He put out his hand, and she obeyed. Now they were alone on the prairie, out of sight of all the others, heading toward the brush-filled defile where they had last seen the black horse. Something began to tug at Hewitt's mind, warning him. He shook his head at the girl and hauled his horse to a stop.

She stopped impatiently, swiveling her mare to face him. "Now what?" she snarled.

"If he's got a chance to pick one or both of us off," he said, "he'd be a fool to pass it up—and this man is not that kind of fool. You know where I think he is? Standing somewhere deep in that brush, resting a tired horse and waiting for us to come into range."

"That sounded like a thirty-thirty to me," she said scornfully, "same as your gun. I'll drill either one of you a hundred and fifty yards beyond the range of that pop-gun."

"Exactly," he said. "So why not use our wits? Drop off your horse. Lean over to examine her forefoot, as though she's going lame. Then start leading her yonder."

She frowned, and looked more beautiful than ever.

"In a firefight," he said, "you've got to fit your plans to your terrain. If he's down in the gully, he's going to lose track of you suddenly. You'll go out of his sight, because

I'm going to be walking my horse very, very carefully straight at him.

"You watch for me, not for him, because you won't be able to see him any more than he can see you. Don't come riding out like a fool the minute I fire. I'll hold up my hat when I think you've got a shot, and then you mount up and ride like hell until you've got him within range."

She nodded, her dark, intelligent eyes sparkling. She dropped out of the saddle, Winchester in hand, and leaned the gun against the mare's body to make her lift her foot. Hewitt pantomimed regret by shaking his head sadly and pointing back toward where they had come from. The girl stroked the mare's leg for a moment, then began walking back, leading her.

Shortly she veered away, and Hewitt began his slow, wary, plodding approach to the deep brush in the gully. He figured he was as good as any man alive with a .30-30, but you had to see your target before you could shoot him.

He heard the shriek of the bullet and then the crack of the rifle and he knew he had come within .30-30 range without seeing the sniper. He did not look back; he had to count on the girl having sense enough to obey orders. He dismounted, patted his horse on the rump, and started it back along the trail, its reins dragging.

He began walking forward slowly, eyes searching the pale greenery of the spring foliage that filled the defile so densely.

He saw the man just as he brought the gun up for another shot. He dropped to his knee, cuddled the Henry to his shoulder, and snapped one quick shot. You knew

when you hit and you knew when you missed, even before it left the barrel.

This time he had hit. The man never got his shot off.
He simply sat down in the brush and fell over on his side,
with his gun across his lap.

"Mr. Hewitt, Mr. Hewitt!" Sabine was calling.

"Stay where you are until I'm sure," he called back. "I
got one of them but I don't think it's the one we want."

He almost ran into the brush, diving into cover, his
heart pounding. He pushed through to where the man lay
where he had fallen. He was dead, shot high in the heart
as Hewitt had known he would be. He leaned down to
turn him over.

A stranger, a gaunt, middle-aged man whose dead face
was still full of rage against the world. A shabby man who
probably had never done an honest day's work in his life,
and now he never would.

Hewitt came out of the brush and called, "Sabine,
catch my horse and bring him to me. We fell for another
decoy, but we got this one."

The girl brought his horse and looked the dead man
over without a sign of emotion showing on her face. She
frowned up at Hewitt.

"The man we want," he said, "is long gone and far
away by now. The shooting will bring our boys up. Now
we rest, that's all. Ever see this fellow before?"

"No," she said, "but since the wagon road opened to the
Qu'Appelle, the country's full of riffraff like this."

It took only a few minutes for Elphinstone and two of
the men to locate them. None of the three had ever seen
the dead man before, but one recognized his .30-30. It

had been stolen less than a month ago from a family he knew, when their house was burgled while they were out repairing fence.

They took the gun and ammunition and left the dead man lying there. They headed south by west, letting Elphinstone lead the way. And shortly Colton Elphinstone came riding to meet them.

"We heard shooting," he said.

"I guess you did," Hewitt replied. "Somebody took a potshot at us and I let him have one back."

"What happened?"

"He fell over," said Hewitt, "and didn't move. We ought to give him decent burial if we can."

"The hell with that," said Colton. "They almost got Constable Hewston. A thirty-thirty slug in the side, and it's sore as hell, but we've got it bandaged up and he's ready to ride again."

"How many of them were there?"

"Three, the Mountie says. The fellow on the black horse was one, but it was the one with the thirty-thirty that shot Hewston."

"Neither he nor his men had a rifle. How did they manage to stand up to one?"

"Mr. Hewitt," said Colton Elphinstone, "you won't believe it, but that damn fool of a Mountie with a bullet in his side yanked out his gun and charged them, and they ran. They ran like rats! And then Hewston just got his horse stopped before he keeled over."

The look on the girl's face was something to remember. Colton turned his horse and they followed him to where Hewston, back on his feet, was preparing to mount up again. Hewitt tossed the .30-30 he had taken from the dead man to one of the men who was riding with the Mountie.

"Sure you're able to make it back to Regina?" he asked.

"Of course he isn't," said Sabine. "Don't be a plain damn fool, please, Mr. Hewitt."

"Oh, Miss Elphinstone, I assure you it's not that serious. Not even very painful. Bit of a nuisance, but we'll make it all right. And see, we still have the black bag with the bonds," said Hewston.

Hewitt glanced at Elphinstone, then said to the Mountie, "But with you wounded, Constable, you're a man short. I think Miss Elphinstone ought to go with you. Give me back the thirty-thirty and let her guard you long-range with her Winchester."

Again, the look on her face . . .

~~~~~~

Long before evening, Louie Fuller led them to where the man on the black horse had joined his four men. They still did not have James Davidson Carlton and whatever loot he still had on him.

But they had reduced the forces against them by one man, and they still had the $265,000 in bonds. The showdown to come was still somewhere between here and Regina, and their job was to keep between Carlton and the wounded Mountie.

"Let's get at it," Hewitt said.

Louie whistled to his tired dog and they put their horses into a trot.

CHAPTER ELEVEN

Jeff Hewitt had ridden with many a posse. Most of them were so badly managed that they were a waste of time and energy, and the first idea of too many range sheriffs was to mount all the idle riffraff available and wear their horses out in the first, useless spurt of hot pursuit. The sheriffs best at organizing and running a pursuit were those with military experience.

Leadership of this one was his responsibility, and he knew he had good men here who knew the country. There was not a man who had not been shocked into realization of this truth by the shooting of Hewston. Nobody with any sense shot a member of the North-West Mounted Police. You had the whole empire falling on you then.

Hewitt sent Louie Fuller out on a swift reconnaissance with the dog, Benedict. "Go like hell!" he urged Louie. "Come back dead on your feet, if you have to, but I want to make sure they haven't slipped off to the south, toward Regina. We'll have snipers out on as long a line as we can command, in ambush, and just sit tight until you get back."

Louie grinned through his tangle of beard. "Iffen you keep between them and Regina, and keep movin' south, you'll have them at your back, but I reckon you've thought of that."

"I've thought of it," said Hewitt, "and any man who lets himself be shot in the back from now on is too dumb to live anyway."

Louie rode off, the dog racing ahead of him. Hewitt sent his men out right and left, with orders to find concealment from which they could observe as much as possible. They had plenty of ammunition and could signal if they found anything.

He and Ralph Elphinstone took cover on the trail a few miles south of where Constable Hewston had been ambushed. It was a well-used trail, but all the traffic was northbound—wandering Indian families, settlers' wagons, and occasional lone riders just enjoying the sight of a huge, beautiful, and still unspoiled country. Most of them had no more than a few dollars in their pockets but all were sure they could take up land and someday be rich. And some of them would make it.

It was almost evening when, distantly, they heard Louie Fuller's ear-splitting whistle and the wild barking of Benedict. Hewitt fired two shots and then, after a pause, two more.

In an hour he had them all together again. Dusk was about to fall. Preston Elphinstone had bagged a deer. They quickly built a fire and cooked and ate their supper, so that the flames could be put out before nightfall.

You had to pay special attention to notice how much useful work Bill Denny did without being told. He gathered wood, stoked the fire, watched the meat. He did not speak, but he was there, the .45 hanging heavily on his hip. And it was Bill Denny who alerted them to the immediate approach of Louie Fuller and his dog, Benedict.

"Ha'n't been nobody got through to the south, you can bet the farm on that," Fuller reported. "I rode for another look at the man you shot, Hewitt. They'd been there."

"The shod horse too?"

"Yep. They didn't bother to bury the booger but they took his coat and boots. Reckon they's scared out of their pants about takin' any more wild chances, but a couple of 'em didn't mean to come out loser. Wish you could see the scurvy pair of boots they left behind."

He had studied the tracks carefully. Not one of the horses was any good except Carlton's black. They all rode native mustangs, and not good ones either.

"I think I found where Carlton run into them," Louie said. "Anyway, four or five had been camped there for a smart spell, livin' on rabbits and prairie chickens and prob'ly plannin' to rob some settler's wagon whilst they dreamed of stickin' up a bank. Ha! You kin hire all you want of that kind for a dollar a day, and you'll still be overpayin' them."

"No matter how good his horse is," Hewitt said thoughtfully, "if he plans to get any good out of his gang, he'll be slowed to the speed of the slowest horse."

"Unless he can steal some better ones."

"Not easy to do," Elphinstone said. "We're not well stocked with good horseflesh yet in Saskatchewan."

"Wal, I'd rather be in my boots than his'n," Louie said.

"Sure about that?" Hewitt asked with a grin. "He could be carrying up to ten thousand in cash on him."

"Where's he goin' to spend it? Ain't no store between

here and Qu'Appelle, an' five hundred dollars would buy their whole stock. The sonofabitch is crazy as a turpentined coyote."

"And all the more dangerous because of it."

"How you figger that?"

"Louie, he can't win. If he had any sense at all, he'd take what he's got on his person, travel alone and only by night, and try to reach the coast. You agree he might be able to get away like that?"

"Sure."

"Can you think of anything else he can do to escape the sure punishment of the North-West Mounted Police?"

"Wal, them stuck-up fellers in their pink coats ain't friends of mine, but by God they'll walk his ass to the North Pole if that's the only way they can get him for shootin' Hewston."

"Exactly. But he's thinking about two hundred sixty-five thousand dollars in bonds, which will probably bring him sixty or seventy thousand in cash if he can get to Europe to fence them. He has neither the guts nor the brains to walk off from that, to save himself."

"It worries me," Elphinstone said, "my daughter, a wounded man, and two others out on the trail with those bonds."

"It doesn't worry me, Mr. Elphinstone," Hewitt said. "The people they meet will respect Hewston's uniform and his wounds. And, if you'll pardon my saying so, I think I let our best man get away when I put your daughter and her Winchester in command of that party."

"She's hardly in command of it," Elphinstone said.

Hewitt merely grinned at him, and in a moment Elphinstone grinned back. Sabine was every inch a lady when it was time to be one; her mother would have taken a strap to her, if necessary, to see to that. Here was a girl who could make her curtsy to the queen empress and add a luster of her own to the occasion. It was a pleasure to imagine it—a white court gown with a train, a small, token tiara on that mass of curly red hair, one circlet of pearls around that tawny throat—

By God, he thought, there's one woman I think I would marry if I had the chance. I could dress her as she should be dressed, take her places even Lord Byrd couldn't go, make her the matron-founder of a mighty new race on this frontier—

And drive her crazy. Destroy her, confuse her, leave her addled for life with the memory of a boy her own age, ripsawed by duty, with only half of her left alive.

Oh no, oh no, oh no!

<hr />

Before daylight the tireless Louie was out scouting with his dog, and this time Preston Elphinstone went with him. The pickets who had been on duty since midnight came in, watered their horses, and stripped off saddles and bridles so that they could eat and roll in the grass and be fresh again.

It took very few orders to form a new, extended line to sweep southward, covering the trail widely between Regina and the Qu'Appelle. This time, Hewitt put Louie in charge on the right, Preston on the left. He let them deploy their men to suit themselves.

He and Ralph Elphinstone stayed close to the main

trail, riding to intercept northbound travelers. Now the
trail was veering sharply westward. A man riding hard
could reach Regina tonight, but they rode slowly, looking
back over their shoulders.

They spared their horses as Carlton and his gang could
not spare their poor bonebags. They kept a sharp eye
ahead for any sign that Constable Hewston had broken
down and the party had made camp. They saw none. Instead, every now and then they made out clearly the
tracks of Sabine's horse.

Elphinstone chuckled. "She's doing that on purpose,
Mr. Hewitt," he said. "Telling us to mind our own business, she's doing fine, thank you."

"I thought that myself, and I don't even know the girl,"
Hewitt said.

They rode together awhile, reminiscing about the
Nueces country in Texas where Elphinstone had ridden
for three years. He had been among the first to round up
the wild longhorns that had multiplied so rapidly for so
many years in the brush there. He and a partner had
collected eighteen hundred head and had built a polewood fence to hold them.

"And then," said Elphinstone, "just as we're ready to
start north, up jumps the devil."

"What devil?"

"He didn't leave his calling card. He'd a dozen men
with him, you know the type, they called themselves
'gunnies' and terrified you with a look. A more poisonous
lot I've never met. Their leader told me he had ridden
with Mosby the raider, and he cited the maxim of war
that his idol employed to reduce the science of combat to
a motto."

"I know. 'Git thar fustest with the mostest.'"

"Quite! He said he was there first and had the most, and he'd thank me to get the hell out of his way and let him have his cattle."

"I don't imagine that's quite what happened."

"No. I like most people. A man has to try hard to make me dislike him. Most of my crew were Mexicans and I'd learned their language a little. My partner happened to be a Negro, and he still had the scars of the whip on his back. Big man, mild-mannered, soft-spoken, but the humbleness of slavery had changed into the humility of a man who was so sure of his own strength that he never had to show a hard edge.

"It was a pitched battle," Elphinstone went on, "because they hit me suddenly while most of my men were out looking for one last crop of stragglers. Harvey—that was my partner's name—and I had planned what we would do if this happened to us. You could almost count on it, if you know that country."

"I've known it for years," said Hewitt. "I never knew it when it was Hell-in-the-Brush, as they called it. But it was hardly a summer resort."

Elphinstone had ridden straight at the leader, yanking out his .45. He was riding a big, powerful, clumsy stud horse that got him "thar fustest with the mostest." Before the leader could get his hands on his weapon, his horse had been ridden down. His gun went flying.

Elphinstone fired twice at one man, once at another. That was the signal—two shots and then one—only it had not really been planned to bring down two men with it.

"In forty minutes it was over. We shot nine of them to death and hanged three," said Elphinstone. "Moved the herd out and left them hanging as a warning. When Harvey and I came back next year for another herd, we were let alone."

"What happened to him?"

"We made four drives and put forty-five thousand dollars each in a bank in Sedalia, Missouri. He remembered a girl he had known who was supposed to be in Minnesota. We shook hands and he left.

"Next thing I got a letter from a lawyer in Minneapolis. Harvey had died of pneumonia and left me everything he owned. Sir Philip's property isn't all I own, Mr. Hewitt. I own the land to the east of him, the land to the north. Sir Philip sold to this confidence man for spite, rather than let me have it for what it was worth."

"How much is it worth to you?"

"To me? A hundred thousand dollars. I hate to say this, and I hope it will go no further, but I've wondered about this deal many a time. Something's wrong somewhere."

"Are you saying Carlton and Sir Philip were in cahoots?"

"No, but I wonder if Sir Philip told everything."

"For instance?"

"If I knew that, I wouldn't be wondering."

They camped early that night because one of the horses showed signs of going lame. They were now very close to Regina, and Hewitt posted his men in a wide arc across the countryside, still hoping to intercept his quarry heading south. There were so many roads and trails to be watched and nobody got much sleep.

Not long after dark they heard gunfire to the west. One shot, then another, then five or six in rapid succession, all from .45s.

And then the unmistakable, hard, flat, echoing crack of a big rifle. Hewitt swung up into the saddle and put his horse into a hard run. He saw others of his men riding in from where they had been doing picket duty.

"Stay where you are," he said. "I'll signal you if you're needed. Don't uncover any trails!"

He rode straight toward where the gunfire had come from. It took him an hour to reach the trouble spot and would have taken longer had not Louie Fuller built a big fire to attract his attention. Louie had been the first to arrive, and had taken command and worked himself into a rage. The man whose horse had gone lame had been told to stay on his feet and use the horse only in an emergency. Instead, he had sat down with his back against a tree and dozed off.

The horse had wandered away. It was the Carlton gang's attempt to catch him that woke him up. He ran silently through the dark and fired without warning—and shot the man out of the saddle with one shot.

Another man loomed up in the darkness. He fired at the flash of the gun, and Hewitt's slightly delinquent picket had the dubious pleasure of hearing a .45 slug whistle within inches of him. He was still firing from behind a tree when Louie Fuller began whooping at his dog in the distance.

The fugitive walked off, leading his horse, before Hewitt's man could locate him. When Hewitt got there, there was one dead body and a set of tracks.

"I think the sonofabitch got through," Fuller said, "and if he did, Carlton did too. They'll be in Regina by morning. Hewitt, we might as well saddle up and ride."

The man who had fallen asleep was almost weeping

with rage and shame. It didn't bother him that he had killed a man. He had seen too many of that kind.

Canada was filling up with riffraff as Texas had twenty years ago. There was no way to keep them out, and Carlton had blundered into a starved and hate-filled gang of the worst sort.

"What do we do now, Mr. Hewitt?" Elphinstone asked.

"Mount up," said Hewitt, "and head for Regina. Let's not hurt the horses, but let's waste no time either. How well do you know the town?"

"Not well, but Louie knows it."

"Then you're going to have to flush Carlton out somewhere," Hewitt said. "And fast, before he can do any more damage."

No one spoke. They were no longer thinking of $265,000 in stolen bonds. They were thinking of a brown-skinned girl with red hair who might or might not have made it to Regina, and who might or might not be safe there if she had.

CHAPTER TWELVE

The brawling, bustling capital of the Northwest Territory was an all-night town, and nobody knew what its population was. The Elphinstones had a house there in the same part of town as Sir Philip Quarles's, only theirs was larger. Elphinstone was obviously a man of affairs as well as one of surprises.

They reached Regina a little after daylight. Elphinstone met a man he knew on the street, and learned that Constable Hewston had been taken to the Elphinstone home rather than to the Mountie barracks or to a hospital. Hewitt held his men together long enough to give them money to buy food with, and their orders.

"Eat first," he said, "and then you know what we're looking for. Temporarily we'll make Mr. Elphinstone's house our headquarters, at least until we get information to take us somewhere else. Stay out of trouble—don't try to arrest anybody—don't shoot it out—either come a-hellin' to tell me or send someone."

The two men who had accompanied Constable Hewston and Sabine were guarding the exterior of the house. They looked exhausted but too angry to rest. They had been so sure their possession of the loot would give them a crack at Carlton! Instead, all they'd had was a tame ride, if a hard one. Hewitt shook hands with both of them and then followed Elphinstone into the house.

It was built of stone masonry with thick walls and deep-set windows—typical Texas construction, except that instead of a flat roof it had a high-pitched one that would shed snow. The front rooms were empty. Elphinstone led the way down a long, wide hall with hardwood parquet floors. This house, with the ten or so acres around it, was worth a bit of money and someday would be worth a fortune.

Sabine heard them and came out of a room. She had obviously been asleep in her clothing. "The doctor was here and he said Ranald's all right," she said resentfully. "He's supposed to sleep and rest, but they're in there now, questioning him, and they put me out of my own house."

"Who put you out?" Elphinstone asked.

"Sir Philip, goddamn him," she said, "and a man named Peckham."

"So he's back, is he?" Elphinstone turned to Hewitt. "Gyles Peckham is superintendent of the North-West Mounted Police. He'd have been *Sir* Gyles long ago except that although he fought the métis in the Riel rebellion, he took their side politically. Any government that ignores the ambitions of a large half-breed population is misgovernment, and this town is full of people who saw Louis Riel hanged."

He knocked on the door. Someone barked, "Who is it, please? We have asked for privacy, dammit!"

Elphinstone tried the knob. The door was locked. "Do you want to open this or shall I kick the goddamn thing in?" he shouted. "Nobody locks my own door against me and my daughter."

Sabine lost her weary look. Sir Philip Quarles opened

the door. "My dear Elphinstone, of course we'd no idea it was you," he said. "And, Mr. Hewitt, how nice to see you! Please do come in."

It was a big room but scantily furnished—a big bed, a commode, and a small dresser. Constable Ranald Hewston was propped up on several pillows, covered by a sheet, but otherwise naked except for the bandages the doctor had put on his wounds. He looked exhausted, and was so pale he was blue around the eyes and the corners of his mouth.

"I'm sorry, Mr. Hewitt," he said in a voice full of misery. "You gave me the easy job and I failed."

"You got the bonds here, didn't you? Our job was to stay between Carlton and Regina, and he got away from us. Constable, we can all be outgunned and that's what happened to you."

He turned to the third man in the room. "I take it you're Superintendent Peckham."

"And you will be Mr. Jefferson Hewitt, of Bankers Bonding and Indemnity Company, and you got one of my men shot," said Gyles Peckham.

He was a small man too, not as small as Sir Philip, but still undersized enough to have been aggressive about it all his life. He had to be in his sixties now, and was lean and hard-faced and grizzled.

"It could be so construed," said Hewitt, accepting the superintendent's brief, hard handclasp. "What the hell do you expect of me? I'm an alien here, the elected leader of a volunteer posse comitatus. I used my best judgment in ordering the constable to get the bonds to Regina as our first duty, and now I'd like to know where the hell they are."

"We stirred Mr. Patterson out and put them in his

Dead Eye

vault," the superintendent said in a less bellicose voice. "Agreed, Mr. Hewitt, you had a hell of a decision to make. But when one of my lads get pinked, I take it as a personal affront."

"So do I. The sonofabitch responsible for all this is an American, and he's still at large, armed, and with God knows how much money on him. I wonder what Constable Hewston could tell you that would be useful in apprehending this man before he kills somebody else."

"Frankly," said Peckham, "I was questioning him about you and your part in this damned case. We had best let him alone to sleep now, while you and I talk."

The four men went out and rode the short distance to Sir Philip's house. There, despite the early hour, a big breakfast awaited them. Franklyn Patterson arrived, panting, in time to share it. He brought with him some telegrams for Hewitt.

The one filed earliest by Conrad merely informed him that New York banks had posted a reward of ten thousand dollars for Carlton, dead or alive. Three hours later Conrad had filed a lengthier wire, which must have caused him agony trying to code it to save money. It said:

QUARTER BUSHEL RESTITUTION LEVEL STOP RITZ
CASHED BEARER BONDS NYC BEFORE DECAMPING STOP
MIDDLEMAN TERRIFIED INTO FLIGHT STOP WAS
TECHNICALLY GUILTY THOUGH PLANNED NOTHING
STOP ESTIMATE SIXTY PER CENT RITZ LOOT
FORGERIES STOP HAVE FIRM FORTY-PER-CENT OFFER
FOR SLICK STIFF PAPER STOP RECALL POSTEN CASE

"Quarter bushel" obviously meant "Peck," who had

been on the "level" about attempting to make restitution with his own funds. It made Hewitt feel better to know that the seedy little man who had died with a knife in his neck, less than ten feet from where Hewitt slept, had been telling the truth.

"Middleman" meant Brewer—the firm was Carlton, *Brewer* and Peck. "Ritz" of course meant "Carlton." Brewer, the poor, weak fool, had discovered Carlton's scheme and had taken flight, and Carlton had gone after him and killed him to shut him up—just as he had gone after Peck and eventually, methodically, killed him too.

And all for a portfolio of bonds, sixty per cent of which were forgeries! "Recall Posten case" was clear enough. Bankers Bonding and Indemnity Company had been called in to audit a firm when several banks became suspicious about the amount of its stock being offered as collateral for loans. An officer in the company had had the stock forged. Very well, there was an insider in this case, too.

And now the railroads, steamship lines, canals, factories, and public-improvement districts whose bonds were among Carlton's loot were in mortal peril. Thus, the firm offer of a forty-per-cent recovery fee for the stolen bonds —*even the forgeries.*

Because the value of *all* the stolen bonds was in question until the watered ones were identified. Rumor could wreck an honestly run company as easily and swiftly as a solid one, once New York's financial pirates organized a selling campaign. Even the biggest ones could not stand a well-planned bear raid. And nothing started such a raid like wild, complex rumor.

The forgers were not Hewitt's concern but the forgeries were. A forty-per-cent reward made the forged bonds more valuable to him than the good ones!

He put the telegrams in his pocket and waited for a break in the conversation. "Gentlemen," he said then, "I'm afraid I have some bad news for a couple of you."

"Who?" Patterson snapped. He was in a bad temper this morning anyway.

"You and Sir Philip. Some of those bonds you bought aren't merely stolen, they're forged."

"*What?*" the banker exclaimed. "The man was a damned thief. Why should he steal forgeries?"

"He didn't know they were forgeries. They're mixed in with the good paper. All the bonds you two hold are evidence badly needed in New York. I urge you to turn them over to Superintendent Peckham at once."

"It doesn't make sense," Peckham said.

Hewitt turned to the superintendent. "Mr. Superintendent," he said, "there's no fool like a thief in a hurry. I doubt he even knows they're forgeries, but some of them certainly are. I've worked cases like this before. We're talking about the credit of every company whose bonds are in Carlton's hands, until the forgeries are identified. If you doubt me, wire your own sources of information in New York."

"I simply can't believe this," Sir Philip said stiffly. "Frankly, Mr. Hewitt, it's an insult to our intelligence."

"Suit yourself. Believe a thief who has already had his hand in your pocket, if you like. I advise you to give Superintendent Peckham the bonds."

"I'll be damned if I will!" said Sir Philip. "They're all I

have, and if they have any value to me, if I can recover a finder's fee—"

"I imagine Superintendent Peckham will have a court order before the day is out," Hewitt said. "One of his constables was shot. That isn't a trivial matter. More than a dozen honest settlers have been fighting a running battle for two days and three nights with an organized gang of thugs run by this same American you knew as McCarthy. That isn't very trivial. You're being asked to trust your own British law, not me."

"I refuse to discuss it further. The whole thing reeks of romantic fiction, Mr. Hewitt."

Hewitt folded his napkin and stood up. "I'm sorry to give offense, but I find myself unable to accept your hospitality further. I'll have to ask you gentlemen to excuse me. Superintendent, and Mr. Patterson—may I call on you later in the day?"

"What's got into you? Refuse to accept my hospitality—dammit, no man I invited to break bread with me has ever been so insulting. Why?"

"Because, Sir Philip," said Hewitt, as he walked toward the chair on which he had put his hat and gun, "your attitude is suspicious. And if you'll accept a word of warning from someone who feels that way, if I were you I would put myself *and those bonds* under the protection of the North-West Mounted Police without another second's delay. If my partner and I can figure this out, so can Carlton."

CHAPTER THIRTEEN

He waited less than an hour at the barracks of the Mounties before Superintendent Peckham appeared. Under his arm was a flat package, on his face a grim look.

"You had better be damned sure of yourself, a lot surer than I think you are," he said.

"Where's Elphinstone?"

"He went to the bank. That's where his bonds are, in the vault."

"Let's get over there with them. I don't think we've got forever."

The $265,000 in bonds brought down by Hewston, Sabine, and the two members of the posse had been taken to the bank earlier. Hewitt, Peckham, Elphinstone, and Patterson locked themselves in the latter's office and went through $345,000 worth of bonds, one at a time.

All of Sir Philip's bonds had been Union Pacific. Elphinstone had New Jersey Steamship Company, Inc., Cardiff and Bristol Steam Lines, Ltd., Pennsylvania-Webb-Hartfield Coal Company, and Buffalo, N.Y., Traction Company.

"All of these," said Patterson, consulting his most recent securities-advisory service, "are big, solid companies. What are we looking for?"

"I'm not sure," Hewitt said. "Let's see."

They started through the $265,000. Halfway through the stack, they came upon thirteen $1,000 bonds and one $10,000 bond of Gibraltar Navigation Company, Ltd. Hewitt slid them across the desk to Patterson and stood up.

"I've never heard of this outfit. See what you can find on them," he said. "I have a hunch it won't be much." He turned to the others. "Mr. Elphinstone, why don't you catch up on your sleep? Superintendent, I've got to send an urgent wire and then I'm at your service, and so are my men."

"I think I'll take you up on that," Elphinstone said. "As the Mexicans say, my bones splinter with fatigue."

The superintendent, still stiffly reserved if not surly, rode with Hewitt to the Canadian Pacific station. There, Hewitt sent his partner a wire at "urgent" rates, saying:

VITAL FORWARD SOONEST ALL ABOUT GIBRALTAR
NAVIGATION CO LTD STOP FOUNDERS COMMA PAST
AND PRESENT DIRECTORS CAPITALIZATION REPUTATION
STOP HUNCH IF ANY OUR CLIENTS OWN NOW IS TIME
TO DUMP

He handed the wire to Peckham to read. The superintendent handed it back with a shrug. "Means less than nothing to me. What's next?"

"As soon as I pay this man," Hewitt said, with a smile at the telegrapher, "there's one other little curiosity I'd like to satisfy."

He prepaid the wire and handed the operator an extra five-dollar gold piece. "Oh, really, I can't accept tips," the man said.

"I tip waiters and bartenders, not professional men,"

said Hewitt. "That's a fee for extra-fast service. There'll be one twice that big if a reply is delivered to the North-West Mounted Police barracks at whatever time of day or night it's received."

"The lines between here and Cheyenne are anything but direct. Even if this is delivered immediately—"

"It will be."

"I could hardly expect a reply before sometime tonight, perhaps close to midnight."

"Could I persuade you to stay open tonight and wait for it? Pay in advance, even if it never comes."

He gave the operator a twenty-dollar bill and left him a little breathless. His salary was probably no more than forty dollars a month, and doubtless nothing like this had ever happened to him before.

Outside the station, Superintendent Peckham said, "Now what?"

"Would there be a copy of *Burke's Peerage* in Regina?"

"One up-to-date one was supplied to me when I was in Ottawa," Peckham said stiffly. "I can assure you that Sir Philip is in it."

"Oh, I never had any doubt of that, but I'll need your guidance in seeking what I do need."

Hewitt's posse had been gathering at the barracks one by one, sleeping in the barn after feeding their horses. Peckham saluted each of them as he went through the barn on the shortcut to his office. "Don't get up, don't get up," he said. "Fighting men must have their rest."

Reaching his office, Peckham got out the big book and they looked up the Quarles family. Sir Philip's grandfather had been the first baronet, winning it under Wellington in India. Sir Philip's father had married the fourth daughter of the Duke of Kilmoganny. Sir Philip was the eldest of seven, the other six being Evan, Patrick, Michael, Charles, Lucy, and Wylie.

Patrick had gone to sea and died seeking a northwest passage. Michael was rector of a church, and Charles was a permanent foreign-office official. Lucy had married Hugh, Lord Vaughan; Wylie was a lieutenant colonel in a regiment of territorial infantry.

"No mention of Evan," said Hewitt, "other than the mere listing of his name."

"Married beneath himself, fell afoul of the law, God knows what."

"Let's keep Evan's name in mind," Hewitt said. "If you don't mind, I'll turn in with my men until darkness. I think the balloon may go up anytime after sunset."

"I'll give you my own chamber."

"No, we irregulars bunk together. I'm sure you'll understand that."

Some of Hewitt's men had found friends they trusted, and had, on their own initiative, offered them jobs with Hewitt. Thus, by eleven that night, a total of twenty-two men, not counting Ralph Elphinstone, had gathered in the stables at the Mountie barracks.

Hewitt liked the looks of all of them. He liked the way they handled their arms and the kind of horses they rode. These were men who had come here to make their fortunes from the first penny up. They had hung around Regina for varying periods of time, asking questions, listening, planning where to take up land.

They were not violent men but they were not afraid of violence if it came to them. He introduced Superintendent Sir Gyles Peckham to them with considerable satisfaction.

"You're on my payroll and you're not policemen," he said, "but you'll take your orders from the superintendent the same as I."

"The first thing we need," said Peckham, "is a good description of our man. So far we're hunting a wraith, a ghost, a man of glass."

"Not at all," said Elphinstone. "Preston and Colton and I saw him. We can give you a good description of him."

"Then let's try something," Hewitt said. "Let's see if we can get a picture of him."

He got out a case containing some sheets of heavy drawing paper and crayons. He also had a pad of cheap scratch paper. Hewitt did not claim to be an artist, but what talent he had, he had worked hard to develop. More than once he had set up in business as a portrait artist as a "cover" on a case, and he had made money at it.

Little by little he brought James Davidson Carlton's face to life from the three Elphinstones' description. Dark skin but not tanned, and somewhat sunburned from its first exposure to the frontier. Black hair that was detectable as a toupee if you took a second look. No mustache, and low sideburns that probably had had the gray dyed.

Wide-set, intelligent eyes, vividly blue in that dark face; a straight, narrow nose; extremely long upper lip and straight, narrow, stern mouth; a small, pointed chin. He stood, the Elphinstones agreed, about five-ten and would weigh around 175.

"We're going to assume," Hewitt said, "that he hasn't visited a barber lately and will try to change his appearance. Or if he does get to a barber, he'll leave a mustache, get rid of his sideburns, and let his hair grow. Let's keep in mind what he *used* to look like, but this probably is more like what we're looking for now."

He had sketched features on scratch paper. Now he put them together on a sheet of drawing paper, leaving a stubble of beard and a short, dark mustache, since the Elphinstones had said he had a heavy beard that he surely had had to shave twice daily to keep up a natty appearance in New York.

"I saw this fellow this evening," said one of the recruits who had just hired on. He looked like a schoolboy, lean and beardless, but Hewitt had the feeling that he could take care of himself.

"Where?" he asked.

"In the People's Supply Store, buying clothes."

"What kind of clothes?" Hewitt could not keep the eagerness out of his voice. "This could be very, very important."

The kid said, "I was tryin' to find a pair of pants I could afford that would fit me. He was just finishin' up. Let's see if I kin remember."

"The People's sell used as well as new clothing," Peckham put in. "I'll wager he bought some used things that won't be too conspicuous."

"Right, sir," said the kid. "Old pair of gray pants, good ones but not new. Couple of old shirts. The one he put on was a gray and black check, and the one he had wrapped up was dark blue. He bought some new drawers and socks and he found himself a pair of used boots that fit him.

"That's one of the reasons I noticed him. He never wore saddle boots before and the high heels kind of tilted him off balance. He bought an old, wore-out hat, I think a U.S. cavalry hat that somebody had dyed black. 'Bout all I kin remember."

"His hair and beard—did they look like this?" Hewitt asked.

"Just exactly."

"All right, let's draw him again. Show me what the check of his shirt looked like, and we'll put its collar on, and his dyed hat. And with high heels, remember, we'll be looking for a man an inch taller."

"Walkin' like a hen tryin' to find a place to lay her egg," the kid said.

He had not noticed where the man had gone. He had paid for his clothing by taking a five-dollar bill out of one pocket and some ones out of another. The merchant had allowed him fifty cents for his old things.

Peckham deployed five of the men to start patrolling Regina at once, looking either for the man or for his black horse. They would return to the barn at midnight and be replaced by five more, who would make the rounds of the all-night taverns until daylight. They would then go off duty and the rest of the men would take charge.

They found the black horse within thirty minutes. Carlton had sold him for one hundred dollars to Douglas Barry, the liveryman, before buying his new clothing. He had left on foot.

"Bet you anything," Hewitt said, "that we get a stolen-horse complaint tonight, too."

The black was a good one but he had been literally ridden into the ground and needed a week's rest and feed. Barry had seen nothing of the remains of Carlton's riffraff crew.

"I don't imagine you're surprised," Peckham said.

"No," said Hewitt. "His job is here and those bums are no good to him from now on. I imagine he has paid them off with a deal for them to go elsewhere."

"I'll wire Moose Jaw and have them look for them there."

There was no one at the telegraph office. Peckham knew where the agent lived, but they met him on the street as he was searching for Hewitt.

Hewitt read the wire from his partner in Cheyenne. It said only:

> BIG QUEENY WILL SUPPLY MEDITERRANEAN
> DATA STOP WATCH HIS FEE

It took a moment to decode. Frugal Conrad could squeeze a code into what looked like an ordinary message and it was a rare occasion when he did not use his full ten words. "Mediterranean" was his way of getting an extra dime's worth out of the telegraph company.

"Big Q" was their identification nickname for Johnny Quillen, head of protection for the Atchison, Topeka and Santa Fe, who was a fine detective with whom Hewitt liked to work. They were friends. Converting "Q" to "Queeny" was just a way of getting "NY" into the wire without paying for an extra word, and it meant that Johnny was in New York on business of his own and would wire Hewitt about Gibraltar Navigation Company, Ltd. "Watch his fee" merely reflected Conrad's concern over money.

Johnny Quillen was well paid by the Santa Fe, and sometimes—*sometimes*—was happy to do Hewitt a favor in return for one Hewitt had done him. But if he got a smell of the bond scandal he would be hard to deal with and his fee could pose a problem.

Hewitt stayed on the street until well after midnight. Peckham had his own men out. They met at intervals at the North-West Mounted Police barracks. No one had seen the man whose crayon portrait now hung on the wall of the superintendent's office.

But neither was there any report of a stolen horse. Hewitt slept restlessly until almost daylight, awakening with a full-grown fear on his face. He dressed and made his way to the superintendent's quarters and had his sleepy orderly stir him out.

"Still no stolen horse?" he asked.

"Not that I know of," Peckham said. "Let's find out."

The officer on watch had no such report. "What do you make of it?" Peckham asked. "You seem upset."

"He'll be well mounted, you can count on it," said Hewitt. "Let's start looking for a dead man, stabbed and hidden away somewhere. And, damn my soul, if we find him, I'll always blame myself for not thinking of it sooner."

They found him within thirty minutes, a well-dressed man in his forties whose body had been dumped in an empty wood-shed. Probably the killer had come up behind him, grabbed him by the head with a bear hug of his left arm, and rammed the knife home in his throat with his right arm.

The dead man's pockets had not been touched. He was a Montana cattleman registered in the best room at the

Victoria Hotel. He carried nearly nine hundred dollars in cash and had been asking about cattle ranges to lease or buy. He had ridden a big brown gelding that was worth a lot of money, which he had kept in the hotel's own stable.

It was gone, and so were its saddle and bridle.

CHAPTER FOURTEEN

Like every frontier town, Regina had its share of
scofflaws, men who delighted in hiding fugitives even
from the North-West Mounted Police. But so thoroughly
had Regina been ransacked that it was obvious that Carlton had left it.

"Not for long, though," Hewitt said. "We don't know
that he knows the bonds are fakes. He'll be camped somewhere within a few hours' ride until he thinks the pursuit
has died down."

"It never will," Suprintendent Peckham said.

"I'd like to take a good look at the bank," said Hewitt.
"How hard would it be to stick it up or burgle it and open
its vault?"

"I'm not an expert on those things. It wouldn't do me
any good to inspect it. I hope you know more about it
than I."

"I probably do," Hewitt replied. "I'm a jack-of-all-
trades and master of none."

"I should think a master detective would be exactly
that," Superintendent Peckham replied. "Mr. Patterson
may be a bit prickly, however. He's of the old school, and
he designed that building himself."

They rode to the bank and tied in front of it. A spring
rainstorm was building—dense, black clouds in the west

and a cool easterly breeze. Now and then lightning flickered in the distance.

Patterson was busy and they had to wait to talk to him in private. "Inspect my bank building?" he said in surprise. "My word, what good will that do?"

"Mr. Patterson, let's just pretend those bonds are good. As far as this thief is concerned, they are. I've covered so many bank cases that I could make burglary a career. If I say your bank is safe, it's safe."

"First you would have to get in through stone masonry walls a foot and a half thick," Patterson said, "and then you've got to open a steel safe that was built for us in London. My God, the bill for getting it here was frightful! That's just how heavy it is."

"Is it a Chalkley and Fiske, by any chance?"

"Yes, but how did you know that?"

"Mr. Patterson," said Hewitt, "may we come back at closing time and look at your safe, and meanwhile look at your building?"

"Certainly, but I think you're unnecessarily concerning yourself. See you at four, gentlemen."

Hewitt and Peckham went out, Hewitt taking his time to look the building over. It was a fortress that could hold out against any but the heaviest guns, at first glance.

But when they walked around the outside of the building, Hewitt shook his head.

"How hard is it to get dynamite here, or even black powder?" he asked.

"Either can be had."

Hewitt pointed to a corner in the rear of the building. "That's soft dirt, and it'll be softer still if we get another rain. Sheer weight in a stone masonry building is a strength only when you've got steel in it. Thirty minutes with a round-pointed shovel there, one stick of dynamite, and you could drive a team of horses through the hole where the wall will collapse."

Peckham merely nodded. They completed their tour of the exterior of the building and saw Patterson watching from a front window as they emerged. He came to the door to speak to them.

"Strongest bank building west of Ottawa and Toronto, won't you agree?" he said.

"Within limitations," said Hewitt, "but it also has the greatest accumulation of valuables west of those cities, too. A wooden building and a railroad safe are good enough for many a sound bank, because they never handle the boodle. The richer the kernel, the more tempting to crack the nut."

"They'll never crack this one," said Patterson with a smile, his good humor completely restored.

"Now," said Hewitt, when Patterson had returned to his desk, "do you know a doctor from whom I could borrow a good, modern stethoscope?"

They returned to the bank at four, just as the clerks were pulling down the blinds and closing the doors for the day. Patterson was waiting impatiently. This, he said, was his afternoon to play whist at his brother-in-law's house, and the highlight of his week.

Hewitt promised not to keep him long. Patterson led him to the door of the safe, which was set into a masonry block in the rear of the room. "You see," he said, "even if a thief got in, he's got a mountain of rock to blast before he even gets to the safe itself."

"Not if he can open the door," Hewitt replied, taking out the stethoscope.

He fitted in the earpieces and placed the cup at the end

of the tube against the green-painted steel above the big brass dial. He began turning the dial slowly, shifting the stethoscope until he found the right spot. Peckham and Patterson watched in silence.

"One thing I would advise," said Hewitt, "is that some light oil be injected into this lock. I can do that for you once I've got it open."

"Once you've got it open!"

"Yes. Like this."

He reached for the brass handle on the latch, pressed down, and pulled open the heavy, six-inch-thick door. For a moment there was complete silence.

Then Patterson said, "I will be eternally and irrevocably goddamned!"

"Mr. Patterson," said Hewitt, "this is where I've got to do a little Yankee bragging. Chalkley and Fiske have been building the same safe for seventy-five years. It's strong, but the only improvements they have ever made in it is to make it still stronger and the lock still bigger.

"That only makes the tumblers easier to hear as you pass their sensitive spot. This bank has been out-of-date for a good burglar for fifty years. I can oil the tumblers to reduce the noise a little, but not enough for a really good burglar."

Patterson took out his big handkerchief and patted his face dry. "Hell!" he said. "Banks all over England use Chalkley and Fiske."

"Yes, and burglars all over England are opening them as though they owned them, once they get inside the building."

"Good God, what am I going to do?"

"M. Stein and Company, in New York, makes a combination lock for a Chalkley and Fiske safe that's as near

burglarproof as any in the world. I can wire them the serial number and they'll have men on their way here to re-
place this one immediately. It will probably cost you a
thousand dollars."

"Let's see you do it again."

"All right, you lock it."

Patterson closed the safe and spun the dial. He tried
the latch and found it solidly locked in position. It
seemed impossible that anything so heavy could be as
vulnerable as Hewitt said.

Yet, when Hewitt, who did not have to use the stethoscope this time, spun the twinkling dial to the combination he had learned, the latch yielded and again the big
door opened.

"Send your wire," Patterson said, and moaned, "but
what the hell am I going to do meanwhile?"

"Place your bank under the protection of the North-
West Mounted Police," Hewitt said. "I think it's worth
keeping a man inside until we've caught Carlton or
you've got your new lock in."

"I need a stiff whiskey," Patterson said. "I should like to
stand treat if my hand is steady enough to pour."

"Not until we have shown you how easily one whole
corner of your building can be destroyed."

It was raining softly when they went outside. Hewitt
was suddenly nervous in the dusk. He showed Patterson
what he had already demonstrated to Peckham. The
banker caved in completely. He asked Peckham to guard
the building twenty-four hours a day and Hewitt to wire
New York to order the M. Stein and Company lock.

Patterson went his own way, probably to a bad, sleep-
less night, since the last thing the superintendent said
was, "I'll post guards around your bank but the dominion

will still hold Volney responsible for that evidence, those fake bombs."

They walked through the rain to the station, where Hewitt sent the wire that might lock the stable after the horse was stolen. They then went to a pub that Peckham liked and had supper and talked police talk.

As they ate, a young man approached their corner table, a piece of paper in his hand. He was not tall, but he was burly of build and plainly as tough as he had to be. He recognized Superintendent Peckham with a nod, that was all.

"Lookin' for Mr. Hewitt, sir," he said, "and I was told he'd prob'ly be with you."

"This is Mr. Hewitt, George," said Peckham. "Jeff, this is Mr. George Bear Sleeping."

Hewitt stood to shake hands with the young métis, a youth with a chip as big as a fireplace backlog on his shoulder. He handed Hewitt the piece of paper, saying, "Madame de Lis says it's important." He gave "Madame" the French pronunciation and his bellicose attitude dared them to make anything of it.

Hewitt opened the note, which was written in a rather large and childish hand, that of a near-illiterate who was trying hard:

Dear Mr. J. Hewitt: I have some important news for you. The bearer will bring you to me safely. Ask Supt. Peckham if I'm to be trusted.

Renée de Lis

Hewitt handed the note to Peckham, who read it in a glance and nodded. "Take her word on anything," he said.

He looked up at the métis. "It's raining like hell, George. Can't you bring her top-buggy?"

"You mean now?"

"The sooner the better, I should think."

George merely nodded, saluted with the same insolence, and walked out.

Peckham chuckled. "Madame de Lis has the one luxurious house of prostitution in Saskatchewan. It would do credit to Paris. Her real name is Myra Schenck and she's pure cockney, but I'd wager that one third of the people on this frontier are using false names. Madame, however, has character, judgment, and wisdom, and within the limits possible, she's my friend and I'm hers."

George Bear Sleeping, he said, was an exceedingly intelligent métis, son of a rascally French embezzler, who had gone to prison, and a young Assiniboin girl. George repudiated everything French and had adopted his Indian heritage completely.

"He's ten years younger than Renée," Peckham said, "and yet she, who pretends to be French, and he who hates the French, are lovers, sweethearts, whatever you like. I like him and I think that under that veneer of impertinence he rather likes me."

They heard the buggy outside, and Hewitt went out to get in. George Bear Sleeping had put on side curtains. The mare between the shafts was a good one, but she did not like the rain and needed a touch of the whip. Yet George carried his right hand in his mackinaw pocket.

"Handle your horse, George," Hewitt said, opening his coat to show the .45 he carried on his belt. "I guarantee I'll get two shots off with this before you can get yours out of your pocket."

George gave no sign that he had heard, but he took the whip and gave the mare a few taps to straighten her out. He turned in through the wide gate of a feed yard—hay and grain for sale—and pulled up behind what appeared to be a row of stores on the ground floor. There was a seedy-looking second story above them, reached by a back stairway.

"Up there," George said, pointing the whip.

Hewitt thanked him, got out, and went up the stairs. The door opened as he reached the landing at the top and a slim, fair, plainly dressed woman wearing thick spectacles said, "Come in quickly, please," and then closed it behind him.

"You're Madame de Lis?" he asked her.

"Her assistant. If you ever need to know my name, it's Delia."

They went into a private apartment at the end of the building, where a buxom blond woman of not much past thirty sat counting money and going over her accounts. In many ways she was quite beautiful, and deeply, unusually sensual-looking. It occurred to Hewitt that she would be a rich feast indeed for a poor half-breed boy like George Bear Sleeping.

"Tell George to wait with the buggy to take Mr. Hewitt wherever he wants to go, Delia," Madame de Lis said, offering her hand.

Hewitt knew it was time to do the right thing plus a little more. He bowed over her hand and kissed the fingers lightly, holding his hat behind him. "Please excuse my appearance, madame," he said. "I've been working long days, and had no right to expect I'd meet someone of your quality."

She loved it. "Call me Renée," she said, "and I'll call you Jeff, how about that? Sit down, and brace yourself, Jeff. There's a thousand-dollar price on your head if they get you tonight."

CHAPTER FIFTEEN

He was not surprised but merely furious, and he was sure it showed in his face. "I don't imagine that's the entire story, madame," he said.

"It almost is. You're not surprised, I take it."

"Not at all. May I borrow your pencil and a sheet of that paper?"

He sketched, as best he could from memory of his previous crayon portrait, the face of James Davidson Carlton. "This the fellow?" he asked.

She nodded. "I don't know the name of the man he set on your trail, but I can describe him, because we don't usually let his kind in here. He flashed a roll of American money and Delia admitted him. About fifty. Not a big man but wiry, tough, fast on his feet. Brown whiskers not shaved for a month. Old gray hat, leather coat, pants about worn out, boots almost as bad. Blue eyes and good teeth."

"You're very observant."

"It's part of the business. He said he was meeting a friend here. Delia put him in the front parlor until that fellow showed up." She pointed to Hewitt's sketch. "I wouldn't want you to think that we eavesdrop on our friends, but this type isn't welcome here and I keep an eye on them."

"You personally heard this offer made?"

"Yes, Delia and I.

'If he's dead before morning I'll hand you one thousand in cash. But if it ever leads back to me, I swear to Christ that I'll kill you before those bastardly Mounties get me.'

"Those were his exact words, Jeff."

"Then what?"

"They wanted girls, but I told them nothing doing, we were all engaged. They wanted to raise some hell, but that's been tried before too. Delia just threatened to call the Mounties, and started out after them. They changed their minds mighty fast then!"

"They left?"

"Yes, but they'll be more anxious than ever to get you now, Jeff. You're welcome to spend the night here, you know."

Hewitt thought it over, drumming his fingertips on her desktop. It would not be the first time he had made a frontier whorehouse his headquarters. The people he hunted ended up there sooner or later—and so did some of the rich men who hired him.

"I may take you up on that until the rain lets up at least," he said, "but there's one thing I would like more."

"The rain's about over anyway," she said. "Why go out and ask for trouble?"

"Because if it's coming, I want to be looking for it in front of me, not behind me."

"Well," she said, "it's sure as hell coming. What's the other thing you want?"

"The whole story, madame."

Her eyes narrowed a little and her face lost some of its cheerful look. "What whole story?"

"I haven't heard of your place at all, and I've been around Regina long enough. That fellow didn't just come up and knock on your door like a book salesman. Who sent him here?"

"No one that I know."

"Madame, I'll say this right to your very beautiful face —you're a damn poor liar. Even if you wanted to tell me— and I think you do—you couldn't safely do it, could you?"

She said nothing, but her blue eyes never left his, and little by little her color seeped away. He let her think it over for a moment.

"Suppose I went to your registrar of deeds tomorrow," he said, "and find out who owns this property, and—"

"It's owned by a trust," she said.

He grinned. "A family trust, no doubt, and Mr. Patterson's bank is the trustee, and of course one couldn't go behind a confidential trusteeship. Thank you for the information, madame, and to the end of your life you can always swear that you told me nothing."

She looked at him, thinking it over. "How the hell do you know?" she asked finally.

"It can't be anybody but Sir Philip. He owns this building, doesn't he?"

"Yes, but don't tell where you found that out."

"I'll keep that in mind. Let me do a little guessing, madame, and you ignore it and let it go in one ear and out the other. Ralph Elphinstone bought the Big C Little c from a fellow who went under the name of Vincent McCarthy, but who was really James Davidson Carlton, a thief and murderer of ghoulish character. The man that

McCarthy, alias Carlton, bought it from was really an absentee owner, wasn't he?"

She said nothing. He went on, "I'm sure Sir Philip planned a big cattle operation there, from the size of the place, right?"

"I don't think I have anything to say to that, Jeff," the woman replied.

"Thank you, madame. You're not merely a real lady but a good scout, and I'll call at the first church when I have time and ask a novena in your behalf."

She laughed. "I'm afraid it'll take more than that."

He had George Bear Sleeping take him back to the pub, where he was told that Superintendent Peckham had returned to the barracks. The rain had been a hard one but brief. Soon the stars would be out. So would the assassin in the old gray hat and leather coat, and he would have no suspicion that Hewitt was looking for him, too.

While he was debating what to do, the Canadian Pacific station agent came hurrying in. "It just came in, Mr. Hewitt," he said, "and my, it's a long one and very complicated. But I had them repeat a couple of times, but I'm sure I got what was sent."

"I have no doubt of it," said Hewitt. "Can I treat you to a beer and something to eat while I read this? There may be an answer necessary, and while I hate to impose on you—"

"Not at all, sir, and a bite and a pint would be most welcome."

Hewitt called a waiter and asked for another lamp, so that he could study Johnny Quillen's wire in privacy, with his back to the wall. He had the telegrapher move around to his left, leaving him a clear view of the door across the table. He did not want any innocent bystanders shot.

Johnny had done an excellent job, as usual:

GIBNAV PVT FIRM NO PUBLIC STOCK BONDS WIDELY
HELD SMALL LOTS SMALL ARISTOCRACY STOP MGNG
DIRECTOR EVEN QUARLES NOW NY STOP THEIR HMS
AEGEAN MESSENGER LIBELED HERE NINTY THOUSAND
BILLS AND WAGES STOP HEAR THEIR BONDS FORGED
IN YOUR CASE STOP QUARLES ARRANGING THIRTY-DAY
LOAN LIFT LIBEL SO SHIP CAN SAIL STOP MAN ON
SPOT COULD PREVENT BUT AM VERY TIRED STOP ALSO
IMPOVERISHED STOP WHAT DO YOU RECOMMEND QMK
                                    JOHN QUILLEN

"There will be an answer," Hewitt said to the telegrapher, "and I'd appreciate it if you could get it on the wire immediately."

To Johnny Quillen he wired:

TIP FEDS AND APPROPRIATE LOAN SOURCES EXPECT
TELEGRAPHIC WARRANT ACROSS BORDER SOONEST THEN
GET GOOD LONG REST STOP HAVE I EVER CHEATED
YOU QMK

The telegrapher hurried off with Hewitt's reply in his hand. A man who looked familiar passed the open door of the pub—which was only half a pub and half a saloon that would not have looked out-of-place in Tombstone, Arizona.

The next time Hewitt saw the man pass, he blew out

the lamp, got up, and hurried to the door. Sure enough, in a moment he saw the man turn half a block down the street and start back.

It was George Bear Sleeping, coatless, and wearing a .45 where he could get at it easily. Leaning in the doorway, Hewitt accosted him.

"Excuse me, Mr. Bear Sleeping, but are you under orders to guard me?"

The métis merely grunted and said, "Yes."

"Why?"

"That bastard ain't a one-man job, Mr. Hewitt."

"Come on! It's always a one-man job. In the end, the man that has been cornered by dozens or hundreds has to pick somebody and shoot it out, and you know that."

"I mean for it to be me."

"How well do you know this town?"

The question surprised George. "Well enough, I guess. No, not good enough either, or I'd've found this bastard by now."

"How much land has Sir Philip got? What's behind his place? Where could a man den up out of the weather, hide a horse, and, I suppose, have grub brought to him?"

"No place on Sir Philip's place. He's got them big green grassy yards all around, and he only keeps one saddle horse and one team, so his stable ain't—"

The métis stopped, jaw dropping.

"Now what?" Hewitt asked.

"By God, that's it, that's it! He bought a nice little farm for an old couple that used to work for him in the old country—you know, ten acres, one horse, some chickens and geese and a hog or two."

"Would the old couple take in a pair of riffraff strangers like this, if Sir Philip asked?"

"No, but Sir Philip built them a new house, and the old cabin still stands at the other end of the property. If he told them a couple of down-and-out men needed shelter, why, the old folks wouldn't even need to see them."

"Come on. Let's see that cabin."

He let George lead the way. It was some six miles from the center of town, on what was called the Old Red River Road, to the American border. There were many small farms along it, and much scent of newly plowed earth just soaked by a healthy spring rain.

Dogs barked. Somewhere a cow lowed for her calf. A flock of sheep got up behind a polewood fence and walked along beside them sociably for a while, the bell on the neck of one old ewe tinkling musically. The blatting of baby lambs deprived of their rest was a homesick-making sound if you had never heard it before.

They left the sheep behind. Where George reined in, a short, level lane led to a small brick house in which no light glimmered. In the starlight it looked neat and well kept, but tiny, very tiny. George pointed.

"Yonder, half a quarter, is the cabin, set back fu'ther from the road. How we gonna do this?"

"Not a bit of cover, is there? Not a tree, not a ditch, not a clump of brush. All right, let's lead the horses off the road, find a place to tie them, and prowl on foot."

The little farm lay on the right. George led the way to the left without bothering to consult Hewitt. Another small house loomed up in the darkness. George dismounted, handed his reins to Hewitt, and went up and rapped sharply on the door.

"Hey, inside! It's me, George. Want to see you a minute."

From inside the house came the angry reply: "Can't do

it, George. Madame would stomp my ass in the ashes if I sold you a drop."

"I don't want nothin' to drink. Goddammit, I want to talk to you and I need a little favor and this is how you treat me."

The door opened and a man appeared, dimly, in his underwear, holding a pistol. "By hell, you *air* sober, ain't you?" he said.

"I tol' you, I took the pledge. Madame made me. Listen, is anybody livin' in the old cabin yander?"

"How would I know?"

"You'd know."

"All right, I've seed two fellers go in and I've seed one of 'em come back and forth. By God, they got their horses *inside* the cabin with them! Now, if you ask me, that means Mountie trouble, and Mountie trouble ain't what I been lookin' for lately."

"Won't be no Mountie trouble. We're just goin' to tie these horses out back of your place for a spell and you won't know nothing about it."

"Yeah, but will Madame? I think I'd ruther have the Mounties on my tail than her."

"She already knows. I'm workin' for her. It's her you're doin' the favor for."

"All right." The man yawned and scratched himself. "Tell you one thing, this feller that goes in and out, he's took the back road mostly past the Elphinstone place, across their northeast corner. He sure is interested in them, for some reason."

Hewitt dismounted quickly and reached for his wallet. He knew he was dealing with a dishonest man, a vendor of illegal liquor, anything but an honest farmer. But he was a man who kept his eyes open. Hewitt took out his wallet and fished out a couple of bills.

"Twenty dollars, two tens," he said. "Describe this man for me, will you?"

"Who be you?"

"You don't want to know. What was he wearing?"

"Gray hat, cowhide coat, how the hell do I know?"

"How close did he come to the Elphinstone place?"

The man's hands closed around the bills as he made up his mind. "I like Ralph Elphinstone, and I like Preston and Colton, and them girls of Ralph's is nice girls. This pryin' bastard sets in that plum thicket and watches that house hour after hour. I know that Ralph's oldest girl is there, and I tell you, what I felt like was givin' him a charge of birdshot where he'd ride belly-down for a while."

"Forget you saw anything. If the Mounties come out here—and they may before morning, if it comes to shooting—tell one of them that Mr. Hewitt said to get Superintendent Peckham out here."

They tied the horses to a strong post and walked on down the road. Then George left it and crouched low as the cabin again came in sight. Hewitt let him lead the way without question.

There was not a sound until they heard the stamping of horses inside the old cabin, and the cursing of a sleepy man whose rest had been disturbed by the noise. They got down on their knees and crawled to within forty feet of the cabin. It was a solid old place with a shed roof, but it couldn't have held more than two tiny rooms.

"Front door leads to the closest room," George whispered, "and the back door to the other one. Horses'll be in the front one. I'll slip around and pound on the back door and then run like hell to cover the front with you. Because if they come out, they'll come out with their horses, that's sure as hell."

"A better idea. How many shots have you got?"

"Six in the gun and fifteen or twenty ca'tridges in my pocket."

"Then don't knock. Just try to find cover and open up. Shoot at the door. Don't say a word, just shoot slowly— just pound away until you've emptied your gun."

"They'll be gone before then," George complained. "They sleep in their clothes and keep their horses saddled."

"Then you won't have to empty your gun, will you? George, nothing is worse than being awakened by slugs from a forty-five whistling through your room. I know! If there's a window, put one through it too."

George chuckled, a sound that conveyed both enjoyment and nervous excitement, then slithered away on his hands and knees. Hewitt counted off the seconds in his mind, as he had long ago learned to do because you could not trust your judgment about time in something like this.

George fired his first one through a window. The boom of the gun in the middle of the night, the tinkle of exploding glass, and the horrified, baritone shrieks of two men caught in a nightmare came all at once.

CHAPTER SIXTEEN

The frightened horses were hard to handle in the small room. George fired again and Hewitt heard the slug rip through the door and thud into a log in the front wall. "You clumsy sonofabitch, get out of my way!" screamed one of the men inside the house.

Hewitt knelt, with the .45 cocked. The moment he saw the front door start to open, he fired, trying to shoot over the man's head.

"Turn to stone right where you are, you sonsofbitches!" he shouted. "You're surrounded. You're coming out with your hands up and—"

The door was flung back and a horse came out with a man swinging into the saddle. He had his left foot in the stirrup and was just swinging his right leg over his mount when Hewitt squeezed off a shot from less than a dozen feet away.

He heard the big slug hit, saw the man collapse, and saw the horse race on in terror, dragging the man by one boot until he came free. The horse raced on. The man did not move.

Silence for a moment. He had no idea which of the two men had tried to break out and which was left in the cabin. Whoever it was, he was having trouble quieting his horse. It did not like being pent up in the small room at best, and for a nervous horse this was anything but the best.

"George," Hewitt called.

"Yo!" came the answer.

"Stay where you are. I'll stay here. If he doesn't come out with his hands up in twenty minutes, we set fire to the cabin."

"Right-o!"

"You bullheaded, iron-jawed bastard," the man in the house was saying to his horse, almost in a whimper. To Hewitt it was clear that he was trying to mount it under the low ceiling, and make a sudden break for it, hanging low over the side of his horse. That meant he had at least spotted Hewitt's position, or else how would he know which was the safe side of the horse?

"One minute," Hewitt called. The man in the cabin stopped fighting the horse. Hewitt waited. "Two minutes," he said loudly. "Can you hear me, George?"

"Hear you clear as a rooster on a hot summer sunrise," George replied cheerfully.

"Three," said Hewitt.

"Mr. Hewitt!" the man inside the house called, and Hewitt's heart leaped. He had shot the would-be hired assassin. The man they had cornered was the coldblooded murderer he had pursued so long.

"Yes, Mr. Carlton?"

"Do you have the North-West Mounted Police with you?" Carlton asked. He seemed quite calm, and he spoke like an intelligent, educated man. In fact, Hewitt thought with a smile, he had the presence of a man who might do very well in the bloodthirsty business of high finance.

"No, we don't," Hewitt replied. "They'll be along

shortly, though. People are edgy, and gunfire in the night —I'm sure you know how it is."

"Then I have a proposition to make you."

"Make it."

"Oh, come, man! We can't stand here shouting at each other for the whole world to hear. This is man to man, just you and I."

"No, I've got a partner at your back door. Any proposition you have to make includes him."

"There isn't that much, not enough to go round for three."

"Then reconcile to cutting yourself out. How much are you carrying?"

"Not enough for three of us, believe me. If you take money you'll have to become a fugitive too, and believe me it's an expensive way to live."

"Do you think you're dealing with Brewer or Peck?" Hewitt said. "Why, God damn you, I just killed my ninth man and it would be a pleasure to make you number ten. You're going to be extradited to the United States and stand trial for two murders."

"Nothing connects me with any murders. I tell you, there's nearly four hundred thousand dollars that—"

"Oh, hell, you're not counting those bonds, are you? Those are all forgeries. Sir Philip's brother dumped waste paper on you."

Silence, while James Davidson Carlton thought it over. Then he said contemptuously, "No bluff ever worked with me, Hewitt, because I'm not a bluffer myself. There are four hundred thousand dollars' worth of high-rate, eight-per-cent bonds that—"

"That is not worth what it cost Evan Quarles at some

shady printing house in New York. All there is is what
you've got on you. You're not even going to get the other
thirty thousand for the ranch you sold Ralph Elphinstone.
He was too smart for you, wasn't he? He had dealt with
smarter crooks than you, that old man had.

"Don't you understand it yet, you damned fool? Part of
the bonds you took were Gibraltar Navigation. That line
is privately owned by the Quarles family. If they had a
dime left, do you think the ship would be standing idle
in New York harbor for lack of ninety thousand to pay the
help and the chandlers' bills?"

"Wait a minute!" Carlton cried. "What are you trying
to tell me? For God's sake? That the Quarles family owns
Gibraltar Navigation? That they forged their own
bonds?"

"Of course they did, and you know why. They're the
smallest outfit of all. They could go bankrupt on hidden
bond forgeries, and the Quarles family could skid out
with God knows how much in cash and security squir-
reled away somewhere. Peck tried to tell you, didn't he?
He knew the bonds of a steamship company that couldn't
pay its bills were no good, and he didn't want your clients' money invested in them."

It was not exactly a guess, because *something* had
tipped Peck off to an enormous embezzlement. He might
not be able to detect an expert forger's work, with so
many bonds on the market and so many engravers and
printers working for so many fine houses producing the
bonds.

But if he had seen his senior partner with Evan Quarles
often enough, he would have looked Quarles up. He

would have found that he was managing director of Gibraltar Navigation Company, which had a ship under ninety thousand dollars' libel in New York harbor.

He might have been a weak man, timid, under the thumb of his dominating senior partner, and unsure of himself at any time. There were men of such deep humility that they simply did not believe in themselves at any crisis that called for confrontation with a more aggressive character. And yet—

The horse shot out through the open door, and Carlton, the city man, struggled to get into the saddle. Hewitt dropped his gun and jumped for the horse's bridle. He caught it, shouting, "George, George, a little help, please!" He hauled the horse back on its haunches and Carlton hit the ground hard and began rolling.

Hewitt let go of the horse and reached for the shot-filled, limber-necked leather sap that he carried this time in his hip pocket. He jumped for Carlton, and Carlton came up holding the knife that was his favorite weapon.

Hewitt did not swing the sap. He snapped it, using the power of his wrist rather than his arm, when Carlton was still on his knees.

He felt the satisfying weight of it on Carlton's head and stepped back like a surgeon who has just made exactly the right incision and knows what will happen next. Carlton dropped inertly to the ground, and Hewitt kicked the knife away in time to keep him from falling on it and perhaps killing himself with his own weapon by accident.

"There's one," Hewitt said to George, pointing to Carlton, "and yonder's the other. He'll be planting material, but this one will come out of it with a headache, is all."

"I didn't unnerstan' all you was sayin' to him," said George, "but I could tell it was really scarin' the hell out'n him and I was ready if he came out the back door."

"And you would have killed him."

"I don't miss shots like that."

"I'm glad he came this way. I want him to live. Your friend where we left the horses—can we count on him calling the Mounties?"

"Somebody will, sure as hell. They won't be long gettin' here."

"Then let's drag this fellow inside and search him and the cabin carefully. I want to get it done before anyone gets here."

In the cabin there was a lantern with coal oil in it. While George lit it, Hewitt used Carlton's own fine, braided leather belt to secure his hands behind him. He used a strong huck towel to tie one of his feet to the heavy, cast-iron cook stove. One thing was sure—when James Davidson Carlton woke up, he was not going anywhere in a hurry.

In a specially tailored vest that he wore next to his skin they found packet after packet of American and British currency, wrapped in oiled paper to protect it from damage from either rain or sweat. It took them a long time to count $46,325.

~~~~~~~

It was three weeks before Hewitt could buy his ticket to New York, where this case would be settled if it ever was settled. For three nights he stayed at the hotel, and then Ralph Elphinstone insisted that he be his guest at his house in town.

"I'm leaving Colton and Sabine here," he said, "but I've got to get back to work. I had planned to buy cattle this year, stocking the place, getting it started for my kids. But I don't feel like investing a dime in it until I know where I stand on title."

"Don't worry about title," Hewitt said. "Sir Philip will execute a new deed directly to you, if necessary."

"No, that's too simple. The lawyers wouldn't like it. I've waited all these years and I can wait a bit longer. But that's home to me, my wife is there, and that's where I want to be."

"I can understand. I suppose Sabine will be seeing Constable Hewston now and then."

"Mr. Hewitt, I never did expect anything to come of that, and I was right. He's a mere boy and he always will be one. He's leaving the Mounted Police to try his luck in Africa. Which brings up something else. What about this young fellow Bill Denny?"

"What about him?"

"He's been coming around to see Sabine, and I get the feeling that they're both serious. And I don't know a damned thing about him."

"I know only what he told me." Hewitt recited Bill Denny's bleak history as Denny himself had told it to him. "I spent quite a bit of time with him. If I had a daughter, I'd be glad to see her married to him. He's short on education but he has everything else to make a good husband."

"Cammy will decide," said Elphinstone. "I hired Denny to work for me up there at the place, and Sabine sent her mother a note by him. Betcha five dollars I can tell you what's in it."

~~~~~~~

Hewitt appeared as a witness before a wigged justice who ruled that Elphinstone's title was good, but who reserved judgment on who should get the thirty thousand dollars he still owed on the Big C Little c. "If it is inseparable from moneys obtained by speculation, as it now appears," he said, "then that must be decided by the appropriate authorities of the state of New York."

Elphinstone put the thirty thousand in the court's custody and received his abstract of title. He could hardly wait to get home.

"Give Bill Denny my best when you get there," Hewitt said, shaking hands with him.

Elphinstone glared at him. "If he's getting *my* best, it's more than he deserves. Mr. Hewitt, it's hard to give one's daughter in marriage to another man, no matter how good."

"I wouldn't know," Hewitt said.

~~~~~~~

The dragging, depressing time was not over for Hewitt, because he had to stay and testify in the hearing on Carlton. The embezzler-murderer seemed to be taking things calmly. Chained by one ankle to the stone wall of his cell, unshaven because Peckham would not let a razor blade in the same jail, he was contemptuous of Hewitt.

"We shall see who goes to prison," he said. "*You* had

custody of *my* money and *my* securities, and I'm going to demand a full accounting of you."

"You keep on feeling that way until you cross the international boundary," Hewitt said. "Then I think I'd start making other plans."

"What plans?"

"Oh . . . learn tatting or embroidery. Anything to pass the time until they trip the gallows."

Carlton said nothing, but he flinched.

Hewitt kept the wires hot to New York, but no word came from Johnny Quillen. Three equally testy wires to his partner finally brought a testy reply:

SETTLE YOUR OWN CASE STOP YOU ARE DEALING
WITH WOLVES STOP ALL EXPENSES NO PAY SO
FAR STOP LUCKY IF YOU BREAK EVEN

The train that would take him eastward left Regina at last. He was in the same car as Superintendent Peckham and the three Mounties who had custody of Carlton as far as Ottawa. Handcuffed, he was chained to one of them twenty-four hours a day. In Ottawa there was another wait until a queen's court heard the case. Peckham presented the pigskin attaché case holding $265,000 in bonds, and a draft on the Volney bank representing the $46,325 in cash found on Carlton at the time of his arrest.

The judge signed the papers for extradition and forwarded them to the office of the governor general. Peckham left his three constables to turn Carlton over to men from the New York attorney general, and left with Hewitt for New York. His testimony was badly needed in the case there.

Also, he would retain custody of the bonds and the

draft until he personally turned them over to the authorities in New York. Before they left Ottawa, the impatient Hewitt wired Johnny Quillen to reserve rooms for them and meet their train.

CHAPTER SEVENTEEN

Quillen saw them descend from the train and hurried down the crowded platform to meet them. "Hidy, Agate Eyes," he said. "I don't care how much of your time you waste, but you've misspent too much of mine."

"You should have had your end of this job done by now," Hewitt said.

He introduced Peckham, and the superintendent and Johnny Quillen took an instant liking to each other. Which was not strange. Both were very good at their jobs, hard workers, good talkers, well traveled. Johnny had engaged three connecting rooms at the hotel for them.

"Only the best for us, Agate Eyes, since it's on your expense account," he said. "We've got a lot of talking to do today, but you've got important social duty this evening."

"What kind of social duty?"

"Remember the Bloodgood case, where you tracked down somebody that got away with an old widow's ten thousand dollars?"

"Fourteen thousand—but what about it?"

"Conrad wired that her granddaughter wants to meet you and thank you. You'll want to bathe and shave and change for tonight, won't you?"

"This is just too damn much," Hewitt snarled. "Conrad knows better, and so do you. Give me her name and address and I'll send a bellboy with a note and make my excuses."

They sat down to lunch in the middle room of their suite, which was Quillen's. The problem with this case, Johnny said as they ate, was the usual one. Companies whose bonds were suspected of being forged, and therefore under pressure on the market, got into a panic and made munificent pledges that they later regretted. And the regrets were deep, in this case.

"The prosecutor caught the forgers," Johnny said, "and got the truth out of them. Only Gibraltar Navigation bonds were forged. And everybody else has suddenly lost interest."

"I don't understand," said Peckham.

"I do," said Hewitt. "These big companies don't mind making enemies of the people who might have bought forged bonds. They don't mind making enemies of anyone when it comes to that. What do they offer, Johnny?"

"Three thousand dollars, total," Johnny said, gritting his teeth.

"I hope you told them to go to hell."

"I did, but the Gibraltar forgeries will have to be turned over to the authorities, you know, and the news released that all the other bonds were good. And there goes your leverage. Who has them now?"

"I do," said Superintendent Peckham, "and my duty is to turn them over to the attorney general of New York, get a receipt, and return home."

"Oh hell," Hewitt said wearily. "Ring for a bellboy, Johnny, like a good fellow."

The bellboy appeared. Hewitt wrote a fairly lengthy note on hotel stationery and sealed it in a hotel envelope.

He gave the boy five dollars, with orders to take a hansom cab and keep the change.

One hour later they were still at the luncheon table, drinking too much coffee and getting nowhere.

"A bluff—sure, I can run a bluff," Johnny pleaded, "but we haven't even got a face card showing. You don't know these Wall Street wolves."

"Don't I?" Hewitt replied.

There was a knock at the door. Quillen opened it to a tall, wide-shouldered, red-faced man whose black hair was shot with gray. He smiled at Hewitt and hurried across to offer his hand.

"Good to see you again, Jeff," he said. "You sounded rather impatient in your note."

"I am rather impatient," said Hewitt. He introduced Quillen and Peckham. "Superintendent Peckham has some official business with you, Al."

"So you've got the boodle, sir," said Al Grogan, shaking hands with Peckham. "I've come to take official possession of some bogus bonds and a bank draft."

"Your move, Superintendent," Hewitt said.

Peckham squinted at him. "I would be delighted to be rid of the damned things," he said, "but my orders are to turn them over to the attorney general."

Detective Lieutenant Aloysius Grogan said, "Of course, I understand. Here is the attorney general's authorization for me to take possession, with the seal of his office. I was also ordered to remind all of you that no word of this is to be released to anyone. The attorney general will make the news known in his own good time, gentlemen."

Peckham studied the document carefully before turning over the pigskin case and the draft. When Grogan opened his coat to tuck the draft away, they saw the .38 pistol he carried in his belt.

He shook hands with all of them before leaving. "Pleasure to work with you again, Jeff," he said. "The department and the A.G. will always remember you with gratitude."

He saluted them smilingly and went out. Johnny Quillen scratched his big chin. "If they're holding up the news on which bonds were forged," he said, "it gives you time to negotiate, doesn't it?"

"It gives you time, Johnny—now you can make your bluff good. Go back there and just hand them a bill and say pay it or *we* release the news. That we've gone as far as we're going with their nonsense."

"I can't do it," said Johnny. "I haven't got your gall."

"You don't need it. All you need is this."

He got another sheet of hotel paper and dictated while Johnny wrote. "I won't appear in it personally until we're in real trouble," Hewitt said. "Keep me in reserve. This, I think, will do the trick."

What Johnny wrote was a simple bill:

Fee to Bankers Bonding & Indemnity Co.	$100,000.00
Fee to J. Quillen	40,000.00
Expenses to 31 volunteer members of posse, payable to and by R. Elphinstone	3,600.00
Total travel expenses in pursuit, due to BB&E, J. Hewitt's expenditure	4,150.31
TOTAL	$147,750.31

"How'd you come up with the thirty-one cents?" Johnny asked.

"Same place I came up with the forty-one hundred fifty

dollars," said Hewitt. "Making out an expense account is an art. Just do the best you can with it. You'll have to let them whittle you down, but don't be afraid to holler. Now, I've got a note to write to that Bloodgood woman. What's her address?"

~~~~~~

He was in the lobby at dark, hungry and impatient because Johnny had not returned. The city looked good to him after all these weeks on the bum and riding the frontier, but Johnny's continued absence made him nervous.

"Excuse me, I wonder if you're Jefferson Hewitt," said a soft, feminine voice behind him.

He turned, snatching off his hat. "Yes, ma'am," he said, "but I'm afraid you have the advantage of me." He took a second look and added, "And that's unfortunate. You—you're not Mrs. Bloodgood's granddaughter?"

She was no schoolgirl. At least thirty, with a full, shapely figure and a lovely round face. Dark eyes, a pile of dark hair under a smart hat and veil. Beautifully gowned, and scented with something expensive that surely had originated in France.

"Yes," she said, "I am, and I couldn't let you leave New York without shaking your hand and thanking you for helping my grandmother. Poor old lady, you got it all back for her and wouldn't take a cent for a fee."

"None was due, ma'am. It was no problem."

"You remember Sheriff Lamb, of course."

"Yes, ma'am."

"He's my uncle. He was in Cheyenne recently and your

partner told him you would be here. He wired that it was my opportunity to express our gratitude. I hope you didn't call at the house today. I've been helping at the hospital until an hour ago."

The hell she had! She had spent a least two hours getting ready for this little scene. "Pooh!" she probably had exclaimed as she ripped his note to shreds, because here was a woman accustomed to having her own way.

"You owe me nothing," he said, "but it would be a pleasure to dine with you. I don't even know your name, though, do I?"

"It's Phoebe, same as my grandmother's. I feel I've known you ever so long. You call me Phoebe and I'll call you Jeff, how's that?"

Johnny Quillen came plunging toward them like a bull, ignoring Hewitt's hasty eye signal: *Not now!* He took off his hat to Phoebe Bloodgood but did not wait to be introduced.

"Agate Eyes," he said, "I've got those people waiting for a quick answer to their counteroffer. They'll pay my forty thousand but only seventy-five thousand to you. They'll pay the posse, but not your travel expenses. And frankly, I just couldn't buck them on that. It was pure fiction and it looked it, damn it! Also, I've got a wire for you from Conrad."

"Where do I sign?" said Hewitt. "You did fine. Of course, while you were cutting our fee you could have cut your own a little, but I'm sure that thought never occurred to you."

Then he turned aside and said, "Miss Bloodgood, let me present—"

"Mrs. Lyman," the woman said, with a dazzling smile. "I'm a widow."

"Mrs. Lyman, let me present Mr. Quillen, a dangerous man with pen and ink," said Hewitt. "Johnny, we'll be late if we don't run along. Didn't you say you have something you want me to sign?"

~~~~~~

Johnny tenderly folded the signed agreement, put it in his pocket, and gave them time to go out and catch a cab. He hurried after them, but then had to wave his hat at the next one.

He gave a Wall Street address and leaned back with a contented sigh. Suddenly he remembered Conrad Meuse's telegram to Hewitt. He took it from his pocket and opened it without a twinge of remorse. It said:

OFFER OF FIVE THOUSAND RECEIVED HERE STOP
RECOMMEND ACCEPTING BUT WILL DO NOTHING UNTIL
I HEAR FROM YOU STOP WHEN YOU DEAL WITH
RAVENING WOLVES ANYTHING IS BETTER THAN
NOTHING STOP REPLY SOONEST

"Even Conrad can't bellyache about this one," Johnny muttered. "That lucky stiff!" He remembered the beautiful woman he had last seen being helped into a cab by Jefferson Hewitt. "That lucky, lucky stiff!" he repeated with a sigh.